ISOLATION

ISOLATION

AN ANTHOLOGY OF NEW HORROR FICTION

EDITED BY ERIC S. BEEBE

POST MORTEM PRESS
CINCINNATI

Anthology Copyright © 2011 by Post Mortem Press
All stories Copyright © 2011 by the respective authors.
Cover Image, *Isolated Damage*, Copyright © 2010 by Eric S. Beebe

All rights reserved.

Post Mortem Press Cincinnati, OH

www.postmortem-press.com

No part of this book may be reproduced in any form or by any electronic or mechanical means including information storage and retrieval systems, without permission in writing from the author. The only exception is by a reviewer, who may quote short excerpts in a review.

This book is a work of fiction. Names, characters, places and incidents are either the product of the author's imagination or are used fictitiously. Any resemblance to actual persons living or dead, events, or locales is entirely coincidental.

SECOND Edition

Printed in the United States of America

ISBN: 978-0615424699

*I'm ashamed of the things I've been put through,
I'm ashamed of the person I am.*

— Ian Curtis

Alone in the Dark
An Introduction to Isolation
Jessica Dwyer

BEING ALONE, IT'S SOMETHING THAT MOST OF US FEEL at one time or another. Isolation and the sense of being separated from the rest of the world is one of the most terrifying of emotions for many of us. The terror of being alone is embedded into our makeup from the dawn of time and mankind's entry into the world.

Far back in the days of tribes and campfires fighting back the shadows this simple truth was taught to us all. We're safer in groups, sticking together means we'll live longer. Going out into the dark by yourself is not going to end well. Any horror movie of the last fifty or more years has taught us that, if nothing else.

But it's not just the horrors outside that we need to worry about, gentle readers. The horror and the darkness that can spring from within us when we only have ourselves for company are just as frightening. When a person is denied the simple contact of another human being or is spurned by the one they once loved, that darkness can rear many an ugly head. Typically those heads contain sharp teeth.

Within these pages you will find those types of lost souls and the causes of their isolation from the world. The terrors of youth are personified in some of the tales. Bullies and broken families give birth to nightmares. Lost loves and bitterness can lead to an apocalypse if you give them the chance. Bad luck finds you in the wrong place at the wrong time alone or perhaps not quite alone.

This collection of stories speaks to the many facets of isolation, of being alone and what it does to us. The horrors that can spring out of that darkness we are warned to not venture into is as infinite as the darkness itself.

JESSICA DWYER

The dread that comes in times such as those described in this volume cause us to cry out for an answer, for a voice other than our own to speak to us. We find ourselves praying to a god that we might not even believe in just in the hope that we truly haven't been abandoned.

But just remember dear reader, when you whisper "Hello?" or send up that lone prayer, be mindful of who or what answers you. You might not like what you find. The darkness and the things that dwell within it are old and have been around since those days of campfires and warnings. And they've been waiting a long time for us to stray from the light.

Jessica Dwyer writes for HorrorHound Magazine, FEARnet, and numerous other websites. She is also the editor of her own webzine, Fangirl Magazine. Her story Red Brew appears in Post Mortem Press' Uncanny Allegories. She's been a fan of dark fantasy and horror all her life due to the influence of Dark Shadows and The Nightstalker at a young age (five years old to be exact.) She prefers her vampires unsparkly and her zombies slow.

Table of Contents

The Reservoir 1
  T.L. Barrett

Conversation on a Dead Cell Phone 23
  Charles A. Muir

In the Rain 27
  Ricky Massengale

Francis 53
  Georgina Morales

Hand Out 65
  Matt Kurtz

**File 8962: Found in Apartment 211
  on Clean-Up Day 2** 77
  Tiffany E. Wilson

Warmth Within thy Depths 81
  Kenneth W. Cain

No Lights 91
  Alex Azar

Insomnia 95
  AA Garrison

THE RESERVOIR
T. L. Barrett

CHARLIE CALDWELL NEVER WANTED TO GO to the Pattenville Reservoir. He most certainly never wanted to go to a church picnic at Pattenville Reservoir; and the idea of going to a church picnic at Pattenville Reservoir with his mother and her boyfriend, Michael Beck, made the twelve-year old sick to his stomach.

First off, Charlie's father, Rob, had told him the Pattenville Reservoir was haunted. Whenever away from the prudent regard of Charlie's mother, Grace Reimer, Rob regaled his son with all kinds of spooky tales. These usually gave Charlie a couple of difficult nights of sleep, but he still asked for them. He loved his Dad; this was just one thing they shared along with a love for monster movies, the Red Sox and fishing. Rob told his son about the reservoir's history on a late afternoon, a month or so into the divorce, on the Connecticut with poles in hand. The story had stuck.

In the 1950's, Central Vermont Power won the rights to a hydro-electric power dam in the northerly stretch of the Connecticut River. Pattenville became the preferred spot among the many petitioned places. Inconveniently, a religious cult had bought up most of the land in a tiny farming village called Pattenville. In the last three decades of the village's existence the Church of They that Sleep had managed to scare away any of the locals that hadn't been happy to sell their land and move. In that time, many people had gone missing, some of them children. When the Essex County sheriff went to investigate, nobody knew anything. With great enthusiasm the sheriff and his men drove out to give the citizens of Pattenville their notice and promissory notes of financial restitution. The village appeared empty. Eventually,

THE RESERVOIR

the state's attorney declared Pattenville abandoned. The dam was finished. Some claimed to have watched the flood waters rise up around the barns, houses, and the village grange. They said the cultists appeared hand-in-hand, chanting to their obscure gods as the waters rose over their legs and bodies.

To this day, what remains of that strange village lies at the bottom of the reservoir. People do not linger there after dark. Occasionally, a tourist disappears in the environs, and inevitably, the power company representatives would find a Saab or a Volkswagen abandoned near the shore with sun tan lotion bottles lying on the seats.

The second reason that Charlie was less than enthusiastic about the outing was that it was a church picnic. Charlie's mother had become ever more religious since Charlie had scarlet fever when he was nine. She had met Michael at such a church picnic. She said it was after the divorce, but Charlie knew better. Rob Caldwell had not been a religious man, and had not understood Grace's sudden and intense re-conversion to her childhood faith. In Charlie's mind it had been the church that had driven his parents apart, and he wanted nothing to do with it.

Even now, the music from a Christian radio station was flooding through the SUV speakers as Michael drove them toward their dreaded destination. Charlie watched the houses thin out as they headed out on Route 13 into Pawanic Township. As a woman shrilly declared her devotion to Jesus in song, Charlie remembered another time when he had heard such a song in their kitchen. Charlie's Uncle Joel had been visiting from Santa Fe. Charlie loved Uncle Joel, who would make up for his daily absence from his nephew's life with spending cash, activities, and a constant stream of funny commentary that would have Charlie and his father doing spit takes at the dinner table. Grace hadn't joined in on much of the laughter. She had a reserve around her brother-in-law which Charlie had assumed was held in protectiveness of Charlie because of Joel's infrequent visits. But as time went on,

Charlie understood that it was because Joel liked to date boys, and Grace did not approve.

Charlie and Joel had been making cookies in the kitchen when a young man singing an ode to Jesus had come over Grace's radio.

"...I feel him above me; I know he's inside me. He fills me with his love..."

"Somebody has got the hots for Jesus," Uncle Joel jibed, elbowing his nephew. Charlie let out a bark of outrageous laughter.

"Get out of my house!" Grace said from the kitchen doorway. Uncle Joel tried to joke his way out of it, but Grace had been adamant. In the end, Joel had left the house with a kiss on Charlie's tear-stained face. Charlie had screamed and slammed a lot of doors, but it wasn't until Rob had gotten back from work when things really heated up.

It was the first real loud argument Charlie had heard his parents have. They both threw things about the house. His father swore quite a bit. It shocked Charlie how few of these fights occurred before Charlie's mother and father sat him down in the living room and gave him the talk that he had guessed was coming.

The final reason for Charlie's growing dread was Michael Beck. A hotel manager for the local Comfort Inn, Michael (He insisted on Charlie calling him Mike; Charlie refused.) had tried to insinuate himself in every aspect of Charlie's life. In everything he did there was the insinuation that he had to make up for what Charlie's father had neglected to do. Most of this had to do with football and Christianity, about both of which Charlie cared nothing.

"Hey, Chuck, Mr. Sanders said he would be bringing his new Jet Ski to the picnic. That'll be fun. I'll talk to him about giving you a try on it. How does that sound?" Charlie had been silent since he lost the argument for coming and returned to his bedroom to find his turtle statuette gone. He had managed to ignore his

THE RESERVOIR

mother's attempts at communication, but he wasn't about to let this stand. Only his father was allowed to call him by that nick name.

"My name isn't Chuck."

The radio announcer explained what fine weather God had provided for the listeners that afternoon.

"No. You're right. Your name is Charles. I can call you that, if you would like, sport." Sport, Big Guy: Charlie shuddered. Michael used these epithets regularly. He was the kind of guy that patted other guys on the bum.

"You shouldn't have taken my turtle," Charlie said. There, it was out. Rob's girlfriend, Ramona had given it to him. Ramona, a willowy woman and a few years older than Charlie's father, wrote poetry and liked skinny dipping and monster movies, which gave her at least one bonus in Charlie's book. Charlie's father lived with her in Montpelier. One evening, Ramona had brought Charlie with her to a dinner party at some hippy friends of hers. They had taken part in a guided meditation to discover their spirit animal. Charlie had been surprised and delighted to find a great turtle surfacing from the deep of his imagination during the meditation. Ramona and her friend had clucked with approval at that. They told him it represented grounded power, imagination, and compassion. Later that night, the hippy's daughter, a skinny girl with beautiful eyes, chased him into a firefly-strewn field and gave Charlie his first kiss. Ramona had given Charlie the turtle to commemorate the magical night. The statuette was five inches long with runic symbols etched under its glazed finish. Charlie had placed it on the corner of his desk, near the head of his bed. He touched it every night before he fell asleep.

"Your mother and I talked about that. We don't have a problem with turtles. We just don't like the idea of that woman introducing satanic practices into our house," Michael said. The first thing that registered was *that woman*. He had heard his mother use the same words to refer to Ramona. Charlie understood that beyond *satanic practices*, whatever that meant, Grace saw Ramona's gift as an attempt to insinuate herself into her son's heart.

"It isn't your house," Charlie said.

"Now, Charlie," Grace spoke up, "we've talked about this. As soon as Mikey can get the settlement in the divorce, we'll get married, and it will be Michael's house, too." Michael often complained about his ex-wife. Charlie wondered what had caused the divorce. He found it hard to believe it was all the fault of the ex-wife. He suspected religion hadn't ruined Michael's marriage. Charlie had seen how Michael whipped a garbage-raiding stray dog and had been wary of the man ever since.

Charlie grunted and reached into his pocket. He pulled out his cell phone and cued up his friend, Mark, on the contact list. Mark had gone to the movies last night, but it had been an R rated movie, thus, Charlie had not been allowed to accompany him. Charlie would see how the movie had been and make sleep-over plans, allowing for this stupid picnic to be blessedly short.

Michael signaled and turned off Route 13 onto a dirt road that wound through a tunnel of birch, spruce, and maple trees.

"Charlie, I want you to promise me that you will at least try to be social when we get there," Grace said. "There will be other kids around your age there, good kids. I want you to promise me you won't talk about any of that weird stuff around them, okay?"

Charlie did not answer. His thumbs flicked over the keypad of his phone.

Michael reached back and snatched the phone from Charlie's fingers.

"Hey, give it back! Mom, make him give it back to me!" Charlie ordered.

"Gracie, the boy was being rude," Michael said.

"Charlie, I don't want you to be texting everyone else in creation while people are right around you. It's rude. I just saw a report about a study on adolescence…" Charlie sighed and turned

THE RESERVOIR

to the window. Michael Beck had taken two things away from Charlie in a span of an hour. Little did Charlie know how important the latter theft would matter after the sun went down.

* * * * *

Charlie was surprised at how many religious nut-jobs had shown up for this picnic on the Pattenville Reservoir. Cars filled the parking area to the left of the dirt road. For a moment Charlie hoped there would be normal people here, too. A quick inspection of all the bumper stickers declaring *Life is Precious*, *Got Faith*, and *God is my Co-pilot*, squashed that hope instantly.

Beyond the people barbecuing and the couple of boats waiting near the launch and the dock, the Pattenville reservoir sparkled in the rays of the early evening summer sun. The area was largely uninhabited. Across the water, Charlie noticed a few forested islands, the wooded banks of the New Hampshire side of the Connecticut and the darker blue rise of the White Mountains against the azure horizon.

A man in an apron came up to the car as they were getting out.

"Michael, Grace, you made it. We can finally begin," he said this with a toothy grin and a grand gesture. "And I see you've brought your little one, Grace. Billy, is it?"

"It's Charlie, Brett. And it's good to see you. Did Pamela come?" Grace said, accepting a hug form Brett Sanders and stepping aside for the two men folk to shake hands.

"Oh, you bet." Sanders turned to Charlie. "Say, Michael here, tells me you're a fishing man. We're going to get the boat out after prayers. Did you bring your pole?"

"No," Charlie said.

"I was telling Charlie that you brought a Jet Ski. I told him you might let him try it," Michael said. Sanders frowned at that and eyed Charlie critically.

"Well, I don't know about that. The boy seems a bit on the smallish side to me. But, hey! There are a lot of kiddos running about the place. Mine are in the commotion somewhere. I'm sure they will be glad to have a new playmate." With that, the two men wandered back to where the smoke rose from the barbecue grills.

"Remember, Charlie, be social," Grace reminded and trotted to keep up with the long-legged men. Disconsolately, Charlie walked down to the shore. He eyed the kids in attendance. Some older teens lounged near the edge of the clearing under some trees. They gave him a sullen inspection and looked away. A slew of smaller kids splashed between the rocks at the water's edge. Only one girl looked to be about Charlie's age. She wore glasses on her round face and a dress that looked like it belonged in an old episode of Little House on the Prairie. From the way that she breathed out of her mouth and twisted her fingers in the side of her dress, Charlie guessed she must have been at least mildly delayed. Her eyes fell upon him and widened with joyful expectation. Charlie's shoulders drooped as he looked out at the sparkling water.

From this vantage point, Charlie could see south to the power dam. Looking north he could see where the river gradually narrowed back to its normal size. He tried to imagine what the area must have looked like before the dam, when the river wound through the farming village. The grass on the river's edge leaned sideways in a little breeze.

Charlie spied an old notched barn beam washed up against the rocks. Big cracks ran up its side from decades of soaking. Charlie leaned over the water to regard it. He put the tip of his sneaker against one end to swing it close against the rocks. Instinctively, Charlie did not want to touch the water itself.

Something had been deeply engraved in the side of the barn beam. It was faint, but Charlie had good eyesight. After inspection, he decided that the carving was actually a picture of some kind. It appeared to be the head of a squid. *Did squids have heads?*

A chubby tow-headed kid splashed up to him.

THE RESERVOIR

"Hey, that's ours. We found it first. We claimed it," The boy sneered and bent to take hold of the beam.

"That's fine," Charlie said and pushed the beam off with his foot. The boy waded deeper to straighten the beam, then made motor boat sounds as he pushed it toward his siblings and friends who played further up the shore.

"Prayer time, everybody!" Sanders shouted. Everyone obediently headed to the grassy spot above the shore and barbecues where the minister waited, a bible in hand. Charlie couldn't remember if the gray-haired scarecrow of a man with ice-blue eyes had come from Alabama or Mississippi.

"Charlie!" Grace called to her son. Charlie pretended he didn't hear her.

"He's fine, Gracie, "Michael said. This was not meant to excuse or ingratiate Charlie, the boy knew that. Michael didn't mind Charlie being out of the circle. Soon everybody held hands; their heads bowed as the minister stepped just inside the circle and began to lead them in a liturgical prayer.

"Our Father, who art in heaven..." the minister began. The rest of the world seemed to be filled with a heavy silence. As the church members droned on in response, Charlie had the sense of being watched. The notion that having a prayer, here, in this awful place, wasn't right struck him. It would draw the attention of something that was here. Charlie looked into the deep, below the sparkling water and took a couple of steps away from the beach.

After the last blessing was cast, and the last Amen was said, the people returned to their preoccupations. One of the women mentioned that they were going to see that the old folks had their share first, and wouldn't it be a good idea if Brett or a couple of the men folk wanted to take some of the younger kids out on the boat for a few minutes.

"Oh, Charlie, why don't you go? It sounds like fun!" Grace shouted to Charlie. Charlie looked up from his waterside reverie and started to shake his head, when Sanders put a hand on his shoulder.

"Come on, Charlie, you get to be one of the first ones out on the water." Sanders manually turned Charlie toward the dock and walked him up to the motor boat where a small fat man stood at the controls. A handful of kids stuffed in life jackets waited inside, grinning.

"Children, this is Charlie. He's a little shy," Sanders announced. "Here, why don't you sit here, beside Rachael? She's about your age. Rachael is quite the reader, aren't you Rachael?" Sanders steered Charlie to the seat beside the plump bespectacled girl Charlie had noticed before. "Rachael here is the church champion at bible verses." Rachael ducked her reddened face and twisted her pudgy digits in the front of her calico dress. She's not semi-retarded, Charlie noted, but she's definitely on the autism spectrum. Ramona had told Charlie that he might make a fine psychologist some day.

The short greasy man started the engine and the children cheered as they drove away from the dock and into the reservoir. Charlie looked back in dismay as the crowd of picnic-goers began to shrink to the size of action figures on the shore. As the boat turned, Charlie tried to keep his line of vision on the shore, but it fell upon the face of Rachael. She stared at him and licked her lips. Charlie looked away.

The short man throttled the engine and the boat lifted a bit from the water. The younger children screamed with delight. Charlie gripped the side rail of the boat and tried to keep himself from shifting against the girl beside him. They passed a couple of islands to their left, turned sharply to the right, and headed out to a great expanse of open water. Rachael fell against Charlie with all of her weight. Her grapefruit-sized breast pushed against his shoulder. Charlie twisted and stood up.

"He stood up! Dad, he stood up!" a kid screamed.

THE RESERVOIR

"Sit down, son!" Sanders shouted. "That's not safe." Charlie sat back down hard. His foot came down on Rachael's toes. She yelped and moved away.

The short man drew the boat closer to the dam side of the reservoir, banked it, and sent out a wide spray of water. The children screamed, and then screamed again, as the man maneuvered the boat into its own wake. The boat leapt and water splashed down on them. For a terrifying moment Charlie was sure that the boat would crash and spill them out into the dark water.

The short man slowed the boat to a drift.

"Now look at that, children," Sanders said. "Look at how beautiful God's creation is." He gestured wide, a can of root beer in his hand.

Charlie noted with dismay that the sun would soon set behind the western hills. The thought of its eventual descent took away his appreciation for the beauty around him. Off to the north, a teenager put up a great spray of water on Sander's Jet Ski. Charlie shivered with the thought of the boy's bare feet so close to the dark waters. He said a silent thanks that Sanders had dubbed him too young for such a thrill.

He leaned over and looked down into that great amber abyss below them. He wished fervently for the hundredth time that day that he could live full time with his dad and Ramona, not just see them on the weekends. He wished he could be anywhere but on this boat, on this reservoir. His reflection on the rippling water showed him a pale face framed by the wavy ginger hair he had inherited from his mother's side.

Suddenly, movement from deeper in the water drew his eye. He followed the movement down to the edge, where the slanted beams of the day's dying light penetrated the deep. Something moved down there, sliding languidly beneath them.

For a second Charlie felt a sense of panicked vertigo and pulled himself back from the edge of the boat. He blinked, righted himself, and peered over the edge once more.

He saw it, or was it them? A string of bony, pale bodies, all in a row, swam fluidly beneath them. The effect was like looking at a long segmented worm, or snake. The serpentine length of bodies twisted. Charlie made out bald pallid heads between these bodies, which bite down against the next body, all one.

"There's somebody down there! There are people down there!" Charlie screamed and pointed at the things that darted whip-like in and out of his vision.

Rachael screamed beside him, got up, and fell against some smaller children on the opposite side of the boat. They all screamed with pain and terror as the large girl flailed against them. Sanders jumped between the driver seats and grabbed Rachael off of them.

"That's enough," he said to the hysterical girl. "Settle down."

"He said there are people down there!" Rachael keened.

"Nonsense; the only things down there are some delicious bass and steel trout. That's what he saw." Sanders put the girl back in her seat, and turned a wary eye on Charlie. He pointed a finger, and Charlie was sure that he was going to get an earful. "Bet you wish you brought your pole and tackle, now, Charlie, huh?" He laughed and went back to his seat. He emptied his root beer and tossed it into a bin.

Charlie turned to look back into the deep. He saw nothing but the beer-colored water descending into darkness. Could he have imagined it? No, he thought. Those things were not fish! He looked to shore where the ant like specks of people talked avidly to one another.

About fifty feet from the boat, toward the picnic, something broke the surface of the water. The thing he had seen before crested up out of the water so quickly and fluidly, it was like catching a glimpse of a water snake or eel. He saw the flash of knobby vertebrae, poking up from the pallid semblance of a human back. This was followed immediately by the shining pate

THE RESERVOIR

of a bald head, which descended into another knobby back. Then it was gone.

"There it is! There it is! Did you see it! People or-" Charlie screamed again. Beside him Rachael covered her head with her meaty arms and let out a great keening wail. As if in litany the other children shrieked in unison.

"That is enough!" Sanders said and rose now in anger. He jumped from his seat and the boat rocked precariously. For a moment Charlie worried that the boat would capsize, then he saw Sanders looming over him. "You'll shut your mouth, boy, if you know what's good for you! Look how you're scaring these children." Sanders grabbed Charlie's shoulder and squeezed, hard. "What is wrong with you?"

"There's something in the water...I swear!"

"Shut it!" The grip on his shoulder tightened painfully. Sander's finger trembled near the bridge of Charlie's nose. Charlie looked away from the bared, baleful eyes of the adult. Sanders held him like that for a long moment, and then pushed against him to stand and make his way back to his seat.

"Man a-live! Really!" Sanders oathed.

"Is that kid...? Is he...?" The fat guy stage whispered.

"He's troubled, that's for sure." Sanders said and then lowered his voice. "But that's what comes from how he was raised. Michael tells me his biological father is living with a pagan." The short fat guy's eyes widened. He turned to give Charlie a circumspect look of pity and horror. Charlie bit his lip and turned to scan the water for the thing he had spied.

"Let's get some grub, Arnie, before it's all gone," Sanders suggested.

Arnie throttled the engine, and they took off for the shore.

When they came toward the dock, Arnie killed the engine. As they drifted in, Charlie scanned the scene and located his mother to be sure that she was safe. Then his eyes fell back in the boat. All of the children were looking at him with open suspicion.

"I don't think you know Jesus," a little girl declared from across the boat.

Charlie's first instinct was to head to the car, sit, sulk, and deal with the consequences later. As he stood safely on ground, the smell of hickory and sizzling meat made him pause. He could always eat, and then complain about a sick stomach with the hopes of a speedy departure. The thought was a hopeful one, as he wandered toward the picnic tables. The shadows had grown across most of the clearing; the sun now filtered through the high trees on the hills behind.

Rob Caldwell had always warned his boy to stay away from the Kool-Aid when his mom had dragged him to these picnics in the past. Charlie wasn't sure what he had meant, but he would stick with cold water just to be sure.

A kid screamed from the water, where a group of eight to ten year olds were swimming and sliding around on the slippery rocks. All heads turned to the water and a woman dropped her potato salad and ran to the water's edge. The child, a chubby girl with pig tails, wailed as two boys helped her limp her way from the water's edge.

The girl buried herself against her mother's front.

"I think something bit her," the smaller of the boys declared, pointing to the girl's heel which was red with blood. All of a sudden the children still near or in the water squealed and thrashed their way toward the shore. Some fell on the rocks, and more wailing joined the girl's.

"She probably cut it on a broken bottle," Michael shouted over the din and wiped his hands on his shorts as he came by Charlie. Michael Beck would often try to regale Charlie and his mother with stories of his past life as a lifeguard and volunteer EMT. He went to the mother who struggled with the child, and led them to a large lawn chair so that the mother could hold the child as Michael inspected the wound. Charlie, curious, drew closer, as Michael held up the foot between two strong fingers.

THE RESERVOIR

"This is a jagged wound. I'm going to need some antiseptic. You'll find some in the back of the Explorer, Grace. Charlie, fetch some of the drinking water," he said. Charlie turned and grasped the cooler from the table and teetered in place for a minute until he found his balance.

When Charlie turned around he saw a very strange thing. The mother held the child in her arms and whispered soothing things in her child's ear. Then, all of a sudden, the girl started shaking all over.

"She's going into shock, Mike!" Sanders shouted. When Mike looked up, the girl lurched upward, pulling her foot from his grasp. She made a loud hissing sound and then struck the mother's head with her own. Charlie winced, the water cooler forgotten in his hands. The mother's eyes closed from the pain. The daughter's head bounced against the mother's shoulder and rolled against the skin at the base of her neck.

Then the mother's screamed, her eyes opening wide. It was difficult to ascertain as to what had just transpired. Then it became horrifically clear.

The girl was biting into the meat just above her mother's collar bone. Blood was flowing down over the woman's flower printed blouse.

"Help me here, someone!" Michael cried. He got to his feet and tried to pull the girl from her mother. Sanders ran past Charlie and brushed him aside. The water cooler slipped from his hands and crashed down on Charlie's sandaled feet. Charlie jumped back from the pain and stumbled against a picnic table. His hand hit the edge of a bowl of potato salad and it flipped over and covered his arm with the mayonnaise rich concoction.

When he focused again on the events on the lawn chair, many more people had gathered around, not knowing what to do. Michael pulled on the child's mid-section and Sanders was leaning over trying to pry the girl's lips apart, or pinch her nostrils shut. The mother's face, seen clearly by Charlie from beyond Sander's back, contorted in a mask of pain and horror. Her mouth was open in a great orgasmic "O", as she trailed out a great whooping scream. Then all of a sudden her eyes changed. They darted to the side and the mouth came together in a large, shark's smile. She bent her neck, darted forward and bit Sanders upon the back. Sanders whole frame shivered with the bite, and he, too, let out a great scream. Now many people shouted and came forward to help their fellow Christians.

Charlie edged away from the mass of people.

"Charlie, where's Michael?" Grace said, coming up beside him. She had her boy friend's first-aid kit in her hands. Charlie, speechless with horror, pointed a finger at the shifting and struggling group. Grace ran forward to help.

"No, mom!" Charlie screamed, too late. Beyond his mother, he saw Michael reach around and slap ineffectually at the mother's head, where she had Sanders in a firm and bloody tooth hold. Sanders twisted his head and bit onto Michael's nose. Then everyone seemed to be there, tugging and pulling. Children scrambled at the legs and torsos of their parents to help.

Charlie ran past Rachael, as she stood and gaped; half of a cookie dangling from her lips. Charlie ran across the parking lot to Michael's SUV. His feet throbbed, but he felt only breathless white terror that filled his mind. He scrambled at the door handle for some time, before his mind registered that it was locked.

He looked inside the SUV, distantly aware of the growing numbers of screams. Underneath the screams, a second rising sound, a hissing, growling cacophony of throaty ululation arose.

Charlie's mother must have locked the SUV out of habit while she hurried to return with the antiseptic. Charlie reached into his pocket and fished around for his cell phone. Coming up empty, he tried another. Only after slapping his own bottom in his haste, did he remember that Michael had taken his cell phone from him before he arrived.

THE RESERVOIR

Charlie turned around. It took him a moment to register what he was seeing. The knot of struggling people had begun to unwind itself. Most of the participants were making rasping, hungry noises. All were covered in blood. Each man, woman, and child was biting onto the back of the person in front of them. They began to move, in perfect unison, unwinding and stretching out, moving toward the people that stood, witless beside the barbecues. Like a centipede it scurried over the ground amazingly quickly, like a zombie conga line from hell in fast forward.

Out of the corner of his eye, Charlie saw an old man make a heroic stand with a barbecue fork before he was grasped and pulled into the body of this new terrible creature. Charlie's eyes focused on his mother, where her hair, bobbed and styled just for the occasion, shook back and forth as she maintained her gruesome bite hold on the woman in front of her. Michael Beck had secured himself behind her. Tears sprang up on Charlie's eyes, and he wiped at them.

He had to think quickly. He dove behind a nearby car and peered around the side. He watched in helpless horror as the remaining folks, flailing kids, and helpless old people struggling with walkers, were overtaken. At the head of the procession was the silver-haired minister. The ice blue eyes of the old man looked on the world in hunger and malice. Behind him, the church organist was fastened to his back, her shirt torn, her great breasts dangling against the minister's back.

The serpentine column of church goers twisted this way and that. The minister sniffed the air. He held his arms outstretched as if calling the flock to worship. He smacked his long fingers against his palms in rhythmic excitement. His arms acted as the antennae for this demonic centipede. He turned the body of the congregation toward the cars.

"We are one in the spirit, we are one in the lord," the creature hissed from the mouth of the minister.

Just at that moment a teenage girl and boy emerged from the trees on the high western side of the clearing. They had probably thought to slip back unnoticed into the picnic after a fumbling dalliance in the bushes. They faltered in their hurried saunter when they saw what approached them. There was nothing in their experience to compare or register the spectacle of their elders and siblings filing toward them in a great rush up the sloping grass.

The girl screamed just as Charlie looked away. He did not have to watch this. He had to find a way to escape. His eyes darted to the road that wound past the slope upon which the creature had ascended. That way led to death. You could not run from something that moved with such unity, such purpose.

Charlie looked to the water. There were the boats. It was worth a try.

He sprinted without thinking out into the open, dodging overturned chairs and walkers as he went. He scrambled onto the boat that he had just left minutes before. He ran to the front and patted down the console like a blind man. He found no key in the ignition. Looking up, his eyes spotted the bright yellow Jet Ski which bobbed against its mooring. Then beyond it, he saw something that made him stop stone-cold still. His terror compounded itself into a great white sheet of brilliance and he fumbled to find something to squeeze with his hands, so afraid he was of disappearing into it.

The aquatic nightmare he had seen before was sliding effortlessly through the water just on the other side of the dock. The world had turned red in the sun's dying light. Charlie's one chance had to be the Jet Ski.

He pulled himself up on the dock and ran back toward the picnic tables. When he got there, he spared one look, and saw the terrible row of church goers descending the slope toward him. Grabbing a plate of hot dogs, Charlie ran toward the water. He tossed them among the rocks at the water's edge.

THE RESERVOIR

"Come and get it!" he managed. "Dinner time!" Then he darted back to the safety of the dock. The aquatic nightmare of boney, molted, connected figures flowed up out of the water and slithered out upon the shore. They hissed from buried mouths their own chant to their ancient gods:

"Phnglui mglw nafh Cthulhu R'lyeh wgah nagl fhtagn!"

The one procession met the other near the shore of the Pattenville reservoir. The minister at the head of the first reared up and hissed at the creature, who also reared its molted head and offered up a spitting threat.

Charlie dropped himself over the edge of the dock and onto the Jet Ski. He quickly set to unclipping the lead that held the Jet Ski moored. He found the ignition and then turned back once more.

The two creatures met with a great fury. The creature at the head of the aquatic procession clawed part of the minister's face off his head. In response, the churchgoers twisted sideways, to better assail their attacker with many arms.

Charlie turned the ignition and lurched forward. He eased off on the ignition and he bumped an elbow hard against the side of the dock. Then he turned slightly and accelerated slowly out into the reservoir.

Charlie applied more pressure to the throttle, anxious to get across the reservoir. What he would do on the other side, he did not know. He would probably dash madly through miles of dark woodland; but he knew Lancaster, Groveton, or Dalton had to be on the other side of those woods, he was never sure which. All he knew was that he wanted to get as far away from the reservoir and those terrible things as fast as he could.

Then he made a terrible mistake - he looked back over his shoulder. A novice at operating an aquatic recreational vehicle, Charlie did not know that he should not do this, as his entire body shifted and his arms turned as he did so. The Jet Ski lurched, banked a great explosion of wet spray, and fell into the drink.

Charlie was submerged a good few moments before he realized that he was still gripping the handlebars. At first his hands would not obey; but finally they relented and Charlie kicked his way to the surface.

Charlie panicked and gripped at the front of the Jet Ski as it bobbed useless in the water. He wasn't going to get that thing righted in the water himself and get it going again. He spun around, every moment fearing the great chasm of space below him. He expected to be snatched from where he bobbed hapless on the dark water.

For a moment Charlie tried to pointlessly heave himself onto the Jet Ski. Finally, he stopped and looked up. He managed to locate the closest land in the twilight. Without waiting another second he began to swim.

Charlie had taken swimming lessons at the local public pool for the past six years. In his terror, all he managed was an awkward lurching flail in the water. Then turning on his back, he breathed more deeply and stared up into the darkening sky.

Swim! He told himself. *You are the turtle! You are the Turtle!* He turned over and started the breast stroke toward the looming shadowy mass of trees that looked so impossibly far away.

Everything became a desperate lunging push toward that shadow which he hoped would be safety. His muscles strained and ached as he heaved himself forward against the dark cold water that seemed to be sapping the very will from him.

In the last gloom of the twilight, Charlie pulled himself up on a bank of wet sand. He dragged himself across some small rocks and headlong into the high grass that grew there. Turning over, he looked up into the shadowy branches of trees with eyes that pulsed with the frantic labor of his heart.

Catching his breath, he let out one plaintive whine of exhausted sorrow.

Movement registered in the periphery of Charlie's senses. He flipped over onto his knees and peered into the darkness. A great

THE RESERVOIR

shape detached itself from the side of a huge sloping rock and moved toward the water. It was easily as long as Charlie himself, but with more mass, more gravity, in the space they shared.

It was only after the creature had slipped into the water and disappeared, that Charlie understood what he had just frightened away.

It was a great big snapping turtle, an old one, a survivor.

"I am the turtle," Charlie reminded himself. "I am the turtle."

Charlie rose up and walked into the bushes and up over a hillock and came back down through some brush onto a shore. He looked across at a great expanse of blackness that stretched out before him. He was on one of the islands on the reservoir. He was trapped.

He moved quickly back into the bushes and tried to spy through the darkness, the way he had come. He saw nothing, but heard the hissing commotion of the creatures quarrelling on the far shore. He hoped they killed each other.

But he could not count on that happening. Nor could he manage the rest of the swim to the New Hampshire shore, not in the darkness. He did not have the strength in him left; he knew it.

So he scaled his way quietly into the sturdiest looking tree and perched there. He strained to listen for the continued conflict on the shores on the other side. As the night wore further into darkness, Charlie began to fantasize that he would last the night, hiding there in the tree. When morning came, so would a couple in a canoe. They would be a little older, maybe professors on vacation, with binoculars: birdwatchers. They would see him waving to them and would come over and take him away from this. They would have warm dry voices. They were Canadians, Charlie decided.

With every tiny sound Charlie would jolt on his branch and he would be filled with doubt for his fantasy ever coming true. He knew when the morning came, if he was still there on that branch, he would have to come down, stretch and attempt the swim across to the other side. His mind could not linger on the thought of that terrible swim. He put it out of mind.

As the night wore on and Charlie shivered, huddled on his branch, he thought of his father. He hoped the thought of seeing him again would be enough to carry him through whatever happened next. After infinite darkness, a touch of light began to filter into his consciousness.

Charlie reached out with his mind for his father, making him his single thought. He hoped with enough will, that his father would hear him, somehow. He prayed that he would come and take him from this awful place.

T. L. Barrett lives with his wife and five children in Vermont's Northeast Kingdom. His weird fiction has been published in many different anthologies and magazines. His dark fantasy novel, The Wardmaster *was published by Post Mortem Press in 2012. You can learn more about T.L. Barrett and his work at: http://tlbarrett.blogspot.com.*

Conversation on a Dead Cell Phone
Charles A. Muir

AT THE GOOSE HOLLOW STATION, Southwest Eighteenth and Jefferson Street, the new rider boarded. Near the front of the train, Siders tied his hair back in a ponytail, watching the man with dull curiosity. The graying, close-cropped hair, cheap leather jacket, and scuffed jeans deepened his ennui in the midst of a colorless afternoon. There had been the usual reading assignments and group discussions in class, and now a twelve-page paper he'd been putting off since midterms due tomorrow: he must describe a process. It reminded him of homework in fifth grade, "paraphrasing" lines out of the encyclopedia about the gross national product of Costa Rica or something.

And this is what I get for putting off grad school for twenty years, he thought, watching the newcomer shuffle cheerily up the aisle. A pointless antipathy to busywork and some guy in a cheap leather jacket sitting beside me.

Siders wedged himself against the window, scowling but not meeting the stranger's eyes directly. There were other seats on the train... all of them, in fact. No doubt it would fill up by the time they reached Beaverton Transit Center and it wouldn't seem so weird that the fellow had chosen the seat next to him. Still, the man's body odor—not to mention his un-American heedlessness of Siders's space—stabbed him with unusual acuteness.
As the Blue Line sailed into the Robertson Tunnel, the man beside Siders began talking.

Into a cell phone. Siders thought he was speaking Russian or Ukrainian maybe, like the babushka'd women he'd hear clucking

CONVERSATION ON A DEAD CELL PHONE

away at each other in the thrift store where he shopped. Without breaking off, the man drew another phone from an inner jacket pocket and directed his speech into that. Shadows wove in his finely salted hair as the train skimmed along the three-mile corridor. The Oregon Zoo... the World Forestry Center... the long, uninterrupted stretch before the Sunset stop. And still the train was empty but for Siders and his fellow passenger, the strange bird chattering back and forth between twin cell phones. Siders started to check his watch but remembered he hadn't worn it today. It felt like an unusually long ride through the tunnel.

The stranger began speaking into a third phone. One in each hand, and the third, or rather first, in his lap. None of them had rung, though their vibrations might have been lost in the hum of the train. A fourth phone appeared. Siders wondered what the rest of the guy's day must be like. Where was he going, what work did he do? How did he get through life holding imaginary conversations on a bunch of dead cell phones? Half-hearted curiosity grew to undisguised admiration as Siders watched the wireless devices pile up in his neighbor's lap, an absurd phallic symbol of defunct electronics. He was counting them when the man reached into an outer jacket pocket and handed him the nineteenth one.

"For you."

Siders took it, not sure if he should. "Hello?"

Dead air, of course.

"Must have hung up," he said, playing along. Another day on the Blue Line, he thought.

"Hello?" he repeated, for fun.

"I'm gonna skin you, little girl," a voice rasped, close and heavy-breathing, "right after you give me a kiss."

Siders scowled at the phone, spat his own expletive into it and thrust it back at the man.

"*Give me a kiss,*" the man spoke again, and seized Siders's ponytail in his fist.

Charles A. Muir

Charles A. Muir lives in the Pacific Northwest. His credits include stories in Cthulhu Sex Magazine, The Willows, Whispers of Wickedness and M-Brane SF.

IN THE RAIN
Ricky Massengale

I

THE HOUSE WAS SUPPOSED TO BE THEIRS; and he would die in it—die happy just to spite her. When she would finally ask how he had died, he wanted them to tell her that it appeared he had died *peacefully* in his sleep. In his house, alone. The weight of the boxes and the unrelenting packed mass of the moving van didn't seem overwhelming, as long as he kept that bitter happiness in front of him.

He didn't know what she was doing right now—didn't care. But that wasn't entirely true, was it? Of course he cared, which is why he was huffing and puffing despite the smile on his face. Who knew what she was doing—cuddling with Mr. IQ? Making shapes out of his pipe smoke while they listened to the soft blues?

Mr. IQ, the man she had been having an affair with over the past year, had told her that the blues "spoke to his melancholy soul." He had told her that before the affair had actually began—if Jackson's time frame was in the right order. If it was in the right order, then this had been about three months before the affair started.

"He says the tenor of the sax is his 'breathless woman,'" Anne had said.

"His breathless woman?" The words had exploded out of Jackson's mouth, spraying mashed potatoes across the TV tray as he laughed. "Breathless woman." This time the words came out clear and dry, despite his laughing.

IN THE RAIN

"Yes," Anne said. She wasn't laughing. She obviously found no humor in Professor Mott's horribly poetic line.

She had only watched him until he became so self-conscious that he choked back the laughter and swallowed it with a big mouthful of Dr. Pepper. Her jaw was set, always the mark of her fury. Little Anne Reynolds of Charleston, Arkansas (who became Anne Taylor, wife of Jackson Taylor), had a short temper and explosive fury. There was no fuse. On their honeymoon, Jackson had been reminded of his childhood, of the bottle rocket wars; there had been a bottle rocket without a fuse, and his brother, the dumber of the Taylor boys, had decided to hold the punk to the cylinder and catch the whole tube on fire. His brother had nearly lost his eye that night, and the bottle rocket wars were never quite the same, with his older brother only watching from the front porch.

Anne was a lot like that bottle rocket without a fuse; and her petite frame only invited someone to try her. What harm could she do? An expensive bottle of champagne and a new hotel room later, the manager of that Queen's Inn Lodge had found out just how much damage this little firecracker could do. When she was furious, the light behind her gray eyes seemed to falter in the shadow of her brows. She had a dark flame in her, and it flickered in the corners of her past.

"Just because you don't understand it," she had said, "doesn't mean you can laugh at it!" As if to accentuate that, she threw her crumpled-up napkin on her plate. He remembered how it landed in corn, and how as she had spoken—hissed—he had watched the corn juice soak into the napkin, as though it were stenographer's paper. Dumbfounded, he listened to the berating tone slither under his skin. "You don't have the words to think like that," she said. "How could you? A high school drop out wouldn't think to be poetic. You don't see beauty in things."

And he had watched the napkin become soggy; in the background, the television was a babble of voices that echoed incoherently in the shocked shell of his mind. It would be another five minutes before he realized that he hadn't been thinking at all, had only been existing, the laughter gone from him.

She was thinking, was going somewhere.

"To you, the woods are beautiful. The lake is. The carpentry is. Everything is to you—except . . . except what's important."

If he had paid attention in class more, he might understand the science of absorption, of how the liquid from a vegetable could seem to climb the woven paper of the napkin. He felt nothing toward the napkin except a stupid assurance that he was looking for something more than there was. Like a man looking at a still-life, he was only seeing it in all its finest details. Meanwhile, another man in his body was being belittled for a crime of which he never knew he was guilty.

He opened his mouth to say something, but she was talking—ranting and crying—and she didn't hear the sound come out of his lips. Most people would have identified him as a big man; the kind of man you would want on your side in a bar fight; his calloused hands had known work since he was ten, when he helped his dad with his masonry. His eyes had squinted for too many summers as he worked on project after project.

"You would never say I was your breathless woman," she finally said.

He looked at her, realizing that he was fractured: a part of him lost in the absorption, part of him dumbstruck, part of him now looking at her. Above her, some distance down, the hall light glowed in its soft globe. It almost silhouetted her, which would have been a blessing, because then he wouldn't have to see the pain etched into her face.

Whatever had just happened, whatever meltdown or explosion—it had been a long time coming. Of course he thought of it like this: of a truck hitching another out of a mud pit. Whatever had snagged that response out of her, its chains had

IN THE RAIN

pulled it from deep within her, had wrenched something out of place.

Fifteen months later, Anne had served him the divorce papers.

He took a break at noon, stood in his new gray kitchen and wondered for the first time just what he thought he was doing.

Three minutes later, sitting on a box marked "Maybe Fragile" in red marker, he scarfed down two fried bologna sandwiches. When he was through with those, he didn't think at all of Anne; that moment had passed. Another would inevitably rise, as a sneeze or a cough would, and then it would pass. When the Anne-moment would rise, he let it play itself out, figuring almost scientifically (for him) that if he did; eventually it would run completely out—like an overplayed tape. At times, those moments fueled him; at others, they killed him.

He remembered his last words to her; they were a prideful mantra at the front of his mind, his own "I think I can, I think I can." When she had traipsed back into their old house with the papers, she had looked beautiful. He had been eating a fried bologna sandwich and watching the news. She had come in the back door, and when he'd turned, he'd realized that he'd never seen her in makeup—not like this—or with glasses. And then her pert little mouth had done something quirky and pinched words had come out, and the papers had fallen on the counter. He signed without acknowledging her painful sighing; and it was only after she left that he realized she had wanted him to look at her, to see what she had become with Mr. Jerry "I.Q." Mott. He had only said a few words, and those words had become his flag that he waved on days that seemed too heavy and gray.

"Anne," he said, and when she had looked back at him: "I've never met a breathless woman."

And then he had walked back into the living room, left her standing there agape, with a smile on his face. He quickly turned on the CD player with a remote and Miles Davis flowed through the emptying house.

Four months out of the divorce, and here he was: a bachelor surrounded by boxed items from a borrowed life. He had left a lot of things at the old house, with a voicemail on Anne's phone saying that she could go ahead and take whatever he had left. He had left the Miles Davis CD on the kitchen table.

It was starting to rain, and the house was gray because he hadn't turned on any lights. And the hardwood floors became dimpled with the windows' dappled surfaces. The boxes took on design. More times than not that spring afternoon, he found himself simply staring at the pylons of his new life.

II

From the bedroom, his bedroom where he would eventually stem a new life, a new marriage, he could look into the backyard. The previous owner (they hadn't cared who had lived there before, Anne had fallen in love with it immediately—she had talked about the flowerbeds she would plant, the grandkids' nursery, the kitchen, how they could make love in his study) had put a metal shed in the backyard, which was normally worth something when it came to selling a house. This particular shed, however, was not one of those favorable bargaining chips, with its rusting sides and misaligned doors.

The rain was blowing into the building's yawning metal mouth, but he didn't care. In a couple of months, in more reliable weather, he would tear it down and build a new one. *So much depends*, he thought, *on a metal shed glazed with rainwater beyond the divorced man.* It was a corruption of a Wallace Stevens' simple poem—which was exactly *why* he had remembered it, because how in the world could *that* have been poetry? Anne was right, he must not see the beauty in things—but it seemed perfectly fine to him. He didn't know what the poem was supposed to mean, didn't care.

IN THE RAIN

That's when it hit him that maybe this was the hardest part. He had been suspicious of the affair; had expected the divorce; but he had not expected the weight of her absence in the new house. What did he expect, though, moving into the house that they had decided on? All of their future happiness, frustration, and hope insulated these walls.

"No," he whispered to the building on the other side of the yard.

This is my house, he thought, but he couldn't say the words. He had the irrational fear that he would hear a voice say *Oh, contraire. C'est le nôtre.* It would be her voice; she had spoken French to simply amaze him sometimes.

He moved from the window, grabbed a box of clothes, and went to the dresser, where, almost absently, he sorted shirts from shorts, underwear from pajamas, shorts from jeans. Inevitably, though, he found himself back at the window, initially looking at the helter-skelter doors, at the rain like saliva on the shed floor, but something else caught his eye immediately.

He had to press his forehead against the cold window to make out more of the stones and wooden frame of what would be the bottom of a cellar door angling under the house. The craftsmanship, he could tell from here, was shoddy—done by a weekend carpenter. How had they missed that when they looked at the house?

And then it came to him: it had been raining the day they viewed the house, so they had decided against touring the outside and settled for looking out the windows. They had seen the tool shed that day, but neither had thought to look down.

So, that's my place, he thought.

III

He waited until the rain had subsided, which took him into the evening. Dusk was settling in a purple haze that haunted the unseen horizon—as though the earth, there, were releasing its tension and frustration. The moon had already finger nailed the sky, and Venus was not far from it. The evening breathed with the post-storm coolness of eroded metal. The metallic tinge always reminded him of being a child, of believing he could fly from tree branches, of shooting bottle rockets under the skin of frozen ponds.

That boy was long gone.

There was enough light for him to survey *his* (that's all it was to him: *his)* cellar.

Although the rain had subsided, the beaded water kept coursing down the green, weather-proofed wood. The color was bright and brilliant, but the workmanship *was* shoddy. The running water dripped between the boards, at the sight of which, he felt a certain disappointment. How many rainy days had poured in there?

He ran his fingers over the smooth paintwork, recognizing the lumps of sealed splinters and knots.

It was a single door, hinged on the left, metallic clasp on the right. No lock. But was he ready for it?

To others, it might be a ridiculous question, one that he might have disregarded as absurd a year ago, but he couldn't even bring a smile to his lips now. There was nothing to laugh about: everything was at stake now. It seemed that the weight of his life, his past marriage, his loneliness, and his future were toppling on the brink of that closed cellar door, into which rain water dripped.

Drip by drip. That was how the ocean was created, right?

He used his shirtsleeve to wipe the water off the stainless steel clasp, which to the builder's credit, was screwed perfectly.

IN THE RAIN

He watched the drips; the drizzling waterfall. Smelled the metallic tinge of something lost; felt the orange, purple sky. And then he went back inside, at which point he began to organize his work schedule.

IV

A new day, a new hope. His stained and worn gloves flopped about his back pocket with each step. He carried a hammer in his left hand—why, he didn't know. It was a "just in case" habit, as was the toolbox in his right.

When he got to the backyard, he didn't so much care for the layout of it at all. It would never do for kids . . . however, a dog, a small or medium breed might enjoy it enough. It was fenced in, and it would have ample running room. Sure, a dog. Why not?

The green door was even more radiant in the day's light. The clasp and hinges sparkled, and he could instantly see some weekend carpenter walking through a nameless hardware store, the hardware gleaming under fluorescent bulbs. The raindrops that had spotted the edifice the day before had dispersed into a fine mist.

The space between the boards, more than obvious in the daylight, revealed the perpendicular bracings underneath. The sunlight exposed that they weren't painted green, only speckled with globs where the color had dripped through. And that, *that* brought a smile to his face.

He could do better than this.

And will, he thought, as he flipped the clasp and swung the door open. It swung smoothly and easily to the ground on the other side.

A comfortable smell permeated up through the narrow staircase, which was also homemade. This house was older probably than he and Anne had originally expected, and that made him love it even more, because if it was something new to him, it was nothing to her. The morning light revealed rigid lines of unsmoothed concrete on each step, descending . . . which ended in water.

The sight stopped his joy.

He had expected water, yes, but not this much water. He laughed out loud, aware that his braying laugh might wake some of the neighbors but not caring. And, yes, he needed that dog. He laughed about the towel on his shoulder, how he had planned to wipe up the water on the stairs, but they were going to need more than that. He laughed more, the sound falling down into the wet crypt beneath this house. He could count ten steps down, and then everything was an unmoving lake beneath.

The cellar hadn't seen just a few stormy days, it had seen decades, which didn't really make sense considering the fresh paint on the cellar door, but there were a lot of things that didn't make sense, weren't there? Like how clouds form, how marriages fall apart, how a husband and wife can become strangers. He sat on the top step and found that it was comfortable and looked down into the cellar. Whatever was there, it was ruined. He was sure of that, and he was sure of something else: he was going to need a pump, which he probably had in the back of his truck, if Matt had returned it.

Sitting there, he was sure of something else. The breed: a golden retriever. It would be an outside dog with inside privileges at night. It could sun all day and lie next to his recliner at night as he watched Letterman. He would drop food on the carpet for her—it would have to be a *her*. Hers were smarter.

IN THE RAIN

V

The pump was small, but effective. It hadn't been in the truck, and he hadn't felt like calling Matt, so he just bought a new one. What did two pumps hurt anyway? He pumped the water to the back alley, where it seemed to become a creek. The small pump cranked and hummed, and the water flowed and flowed, widening until the alley glistened with the stream. And still, after an hour, only another step was revealed. So, eleven steps, now—but how many were there? Fourteen? Fifteen?

While the pump pumped, he unboxed items. He seemed refueled, working through boxes without any sign of slowing down. By midday, the kitchen was in order, the bedroom was nearly there, and there were thirteen steps. There was still no sign of the bottom, and he realized that the cellar might have to be a lot deeper than he had originally expected if the house was on a cement pad, which it was: the cellar had been an addition, and so whoever built it had had to dig beneath that foundation.

By three, there were enough collapsed boxes in the living room, which consisted of his two recliners, the couch, and the TV, that he couldn't stand it. If he kept going, he would be able to clear this moving junk in another day or so. By three, also, the pump had clogged.

Rather than unclog the pump, he switched it off, satisfied with the off-brand gizmo's day's work. There were fourteen steps, at least. A day's work, though, and to only reveal four more steps meant that the cellar had to be bigger than he had originally expected.

So, with waders on, he went down the watery steps—not only to grab the pump that he had gently *dropped* in but to see what he could. It seemed impossible that the water would be more than chest-high.

He *did* hurry from his front door to the back, because he was aware of how ridiculous he must look in his waders without a lake around. *That's 'cause they haven't seen my lake*, he thought, but was too exhausted to enjoy the humor of it himself.

VI

The water was still waist high; and the ceiling gave several feet of murky, cold clearance. There was no overhead light—he had expected, at worst, a single bulb suspended by its cord.

The water was freezing, his fingertips told him that, and the dark cellar was less than he had imagined. It was vast, but that was all it was. Against the far wall, he could make out the pale shape of a long worktable, complete with overhead shelving. There didn't appear to be much else for the amount of room, which seemed to encompass half the depth of the house.

The cellar smelled putrid. His dad would have probably called it *skunk water*—his term for water that had sat too long and begun to develop its own stench. It was a cold, decaying smell. A smell, he thought, like rust and old dirt.

The floor itself, he could tell from the suction on his boots' soles, was packed dirt—which wasn't so packed anymore.

His optimism had subsided. There was nothing worth anything down here, but what had he expected? To—

Something underwater tapped his leg . . . twice.

It made him jump and scream the way a man will scream when he catches his reflection in a dark mirror when he is supposed to be alone. The suction of the muddy floor kept him glued as closely to the cellar floor as possible. It did nothing, however, to keep him in the water. In his fear, he seemed to suddenly hover backward several feet and was standing on the dry twelfth step before he could finish his thought that there was something in the water.

Except for the subtle disturbance he had caused in the vast cellar, concentric circles that widened out of his limited perspective of the narrow opening until they finally lapped at the far walls, nothing moved across the surface of the water. Nothing broke the surface. Nothing.

Maybe he had imagined it. But, his heart in his temples, he knew he hadn't. He had felt a clear tapping on the rubber walls of his waders. Like minnows in a bucket that crash against your hand; like a cat pushing against your hand for comfort. Except he didn't have the instinctive peace of either of those images; he was terrified.

He couldn't explain the emotion, or where it had originated, but he didn't care to explain it. His normal amount of courage seemed a scarce notion. Tensely, he sat on the twelfth stair, with enough footing about him that if something did emerge from the water he could bolt up the stairs, slamming the brilliant green door behind him.

VII

He fell asleep on the couch that night. Fell? Pulled was more like it. One moment, he was watching Letterman, and when he blinked, Letterman's joke had been punch lined by a Tide commercial, which, a blink later, had been Letterman again. He came in and out of consciousness at first, surfacing like a drowning man, with each televised uproar or clapping or laughing. Letterman's voice lost its distinction: it became the drone of a stupid locust and his laugh was like a whipped dog—

And he would find himself thinking, *someone really should help that dog*, as he tumbled through the rabbit hole into the cellar. The cellar, except not yet - he had been there for only a second. And then he had awoken from its murky shadows, aware only that there *had* been light down there . . . and something moving. Now, he was standing in the backyard.

The green cellar door, looking like it opened into the earth, glistened like fresh grass, except it was greener than the grass around it. It was brilliant. *It was made to be seen*, he thought. And in his dream, he was smiling, and he knew that he would always smile, because in his dream, he was free of everything. And this was a dream, right? It had to be.

Somewhere a few yards away, a dog was whining (and he turned over in his sleep). Somewhere else, something crashed and clambered, a tiny thundering noise (and he moaned in his sleep at their applause). It came to him then, in his dream, that it was in fact a dream, and somewhere far, far away, like a kite on the end of a string, he was dozing inside. So, what if he walked through the front door of the house? Would he see himself sleeping?

Cool it, he told himself, still smiling. *Might not be a dream, though. It feels* wrong *for that, right? Too much . . . clarity. Too much connection to that other "end of the string." Here, you're the kite.*

Whatever that meant, he didn't care. All he cared about was getting in that cellar door. But before he did, he looked up at the beautiful spring morning; it was all wrong. The sun was shining, and twinkling beyond its radiance, he could see all the stars of the night sky. Clear as a winter night, the Big Dipper was stretched over him, distinguishable. The Milky Way was also beyond the brilliant blue like a pink watermark. That's what it took for the smile to fall from his face. The trees surrounding his yard were too tall to see much else, but he knew that if they weren't there, he would see the moon and the sun facing for a duel.

Not here, my good friend. That was the Mr. Calm and Collected voice again, speaking from within but seeming connected to something beyond him at this moment. *Those there are only the symbols you understand.*

He actually said, "What?" out loud to the fresh morning. In his sleep on the couch, it came out as a mumble. He (as he thought of himself, the one standing in the yard) was suddenly aware of that other self on the couch, of its lips moving with sound, of the TV in the background. That was there, though, and he was here in this strange *where*.

IN THE RAIN

He looked at the sky again—it was bizarrely beautiful—and then walked to the cellar door, wanting to grasp that clasp more than anything right now. There was another urge, though, that told him he shouldn't mess with the clasp. It should continue to just lay there.

This is why you're here, his Mr. Calm said.

He stood in the morning light, feeling the wet grass soak through his socks—furthermore, feeling his toes squeegee against one another when he flicked them back and forth—trying to understand that last statement. He was here for the cellar? If that were so, then why did he feel such trepidation? Was he here to see *not* to bother with the cellar? The way teenagers were shown movies and pictures of drunk drivers: Don't Do This, Or This Blah-Blah-Blah.

On the other side of the cellar door, the sound was unmistakable: there was someone or something down there. And suddenly, he *was* afraid.

He, though, still found himself smiling stupidly in this *other where* that was *not* a dream. His sleeping self was dreaming something else, and he, at this moment, was just merely tapped into that same self, like a conference call. This *other self* (the one he believed to truly be him) was hidden. The other two didn't know he was here. He thought about his dad's first house (well, trailer) up on the mountain, where the telephones had been different. They had been on a party-line, which meant that before he could call his mom, he would have to pick up the phone to make sure no one else was talking. There were two older women that always seemed to be talking, Mrs. Harrison and Ms. Stobaugh. When he was bored, he would sometimes pick up the phone—quietly—and listen to them gab about people he didn't know. He had found a guilty pleasure in being that hidden ear. It was his own innocent voyeuristic act that got him through the rough days of his parents' divorce. If he wanted to be lost in a world, he chose that telephone world, where he was silently essential.

Now, he was the third entity on a party-line that ran through his corporal body.

He moved toward the cellar door, aware that he was supposed to see what was on the other side of the door, whether he wanted to or not. *In there* was meant for him. It was probably the same sensation that bank robbers felt; the certainty that all of their lives had moved them to this one moment, to enter this unenterable place.

Watching his right hand reach out, the lucidity of the dream heightened, and he had a moment where he realized his hand was rising above his sleeping body on the couch. Reality, he felt, had grasped his suspended hand instantly and was using it to reel him—

(Something started pounding in the cellar. knocking, or hammering. What's more: he could hear the hidden someone/something on the other side of the door sloshing and crashing in the water. hard, liquid sounds.)

—back to the couch, back to the golden living room with dust motes swirling in bars of light shifting through the mini blinds, back to the worn-out couch that smelled like him and Anne, smelled like her here and him there. And when he rolled, it was them together until he couldn't smell himself or her anymore but the dirty foam again. Back to the world—

(Sloshing again. Grunting.)

—with the sunken cellar.

When he woke, his arm wasn't above him in the air; it was laying across his chest. The last image—

(color)

—was still fading, like a Polaroid in reverse. The green doors and the silver hinges evanesced but still seemed to demand their permanence was undeniable, as was the fact that in his dream there had been something in the cellar.

IN THE RAIN

The pounding reverberated again, but it wasn't coming from the cellar. It was coming from the front door.

"I know you're not drunk," a familiar voice bellowed from the other side of the front door, "and I know you're not with someone."

Matt pounded on the door again, and Jackson realized with perfect conviction that there was nothing hidden in dreams. Dreams were only the cycling of discarded images that demanded one last showing. And Matt was his pounding at the cellar door; the wall between his dream and the living room had been too thin.

Jackson wanted to shout for Matt to shut up, but the doorbell was ringing now. And ringing and ringing. The best Jackson managed was a hard fist against the wall next to him, which got the message through.

"All right then, hurry up." Matt's voice was muffled on the other side of the door, but it was familiar and friendly, which is exactly what Jackson needed. "I'll wait right here, boss."

VIII

"Well, boss, you're right," Matt said, looking down into the murk of the cellar. "*That* is one flooded cellar."

"That's why I keep you around: good for the obvious."

There was silence between them that had once been awkward but was now comfortable. The silence was the way they accepted things; in this case . . . a flooded cellar, but did he dare tell Matt that he thought something was living down there? The idea itself was humorous even to him; although he couldn't quite explain why.

He also, now that he was looking at it, couldn't explain how the water had filled back up to cover the steps he had cleared yesterday. It hit him as a personal defeat; something that stopped whatever hope had been lurking there. Had it rained last night?

"But you say you went down there?"

Jackson heard himself say, yes, he had, yesterday, but it wasn't right. None of it was. It hadn't rained last night; he was sure of it. The forecast had been clear; well, thirty percent, but in Arkansas that was as good as zero percent. It hadn't rained, and yet, he was sitting there counting down the steps over and over, wondering if he hadn't miscounted yesterday.

"Anything worthwhile down there? All waterlogged and rotten?"

Something down there is *rotten*, he thought, but said, "Can't tell just yet, but probably. Yeah. I mean," he was finding his rhythm again, finding his pattern like a needle finding its track in a record

(What happened to that Miles Davis record that you played that night? Ever wonder what happens to a record submerged in water?)

Something had flopped in the cellar . . . hadn't it? Jackson looked at Matt, who was looking at the neighbors' yards. Jackson looked back at the cellar, expecting to see the concentric circles come lapping at the stone steps; he could still hear the splash echoing in his head, not the sound of a tail hitting the water but of something falling—

"Jack, man, you okay?" Matt placed his hand on Jackson's shoulder, and Jackson felt the immediate strength in that hand and was suddenly aware of how weak he was. Of how far away. Far, far away. Those green doors seemed. And so, so green. Matt's voice, green, saying, "You don't

(Something falling in. diving.)

(What is happening to me?)

look

(It was *pounding in the cellar. heard it moving.)*

(What's happening . . . what?)

so

(so green. so much water. so weird.)

good . . . Boss!"

IN THE RAIN

And then he was back, Matt standing in front of him, holding him up by both of his shoulders, and his own cheek stinging. He tried to raise a hand to his cheek, but Matt's arms blocked the route, and at this point, Matt hadn't realized that it was time to let him go. As for Matt, Jackson had never seen Matt wear so frightened an expression . . . or noticed that Matt's nose was a little crooked.

"Boss, come on. Geez." He shook Jackson like a ragdoll in his powerful arms.

He wanted to say something more; no, he wanted to ask something: what had just happened? But he hadn't needed to. When Matt's mouth opened, words spilled out in one explosive breath; it was funny how he started, though:

"Geez, I thought you were going to fall into the water. Dive head-first . . ."

And that was funny, wasn't it? Sure it was - because he wouldn't be the only thing swimming down there. He was sure of that. There was a certainty in that that felt *right*. He only stood there, though, listening to Matt talk about how his eyes had started to roll back

(What is *happening here?)*

(It's my place)

and how he had thought that boss-man was seizing—if he did that and swallowed his tongue what was Matt supposed to do? Something with his finger hooked, right? What if, though, he had fallen, then what, boss? Then, what? You ever seize like that? Ever?

Jackson felt like the wind could lift and carry him to Mount Petit Jean, felt like the grass could unstable him. He felt very simply, *light* and comfortable. And inside him, deep within, there was a rational part screaming that things weren't right. Where was the warden? The time keeper? The watchman? This was all okay?

Sure it was.

"Never," Jackson finally heard himself say—pretty sure he was smiling, "and I don't know why it just happened."

Except he did, maybe. He had gone down the rabbit hole, had stumbled upon a trail he hadn't known existed, and had tripped right down the hole.

"All I know," he said, "is that I definitely didn't want to crash down those stairs."

"No kiddin'," Matt said, wiping sweat from his brow. There was a beat of silence, and then he said, "Who'd pay me, then?"

They both laughed, and dang, did it feel good. The ratchet of their sounds seemed to sew Jackson's existence back to the fabric of reality. Only when the tears came did they try to stop laughing, but there were only more tears and more laughter when they observed how ridiculous the other looked

IX

Alone now, Jackson sat at the top of the cellar stairs and looked at the unmoving water. Masked by the bulk and shadow of his house, the rest of the world moved oblivious to and of him. He was alone. His feet rested on the top step, and if he moved, it was only to lean a little further into the mouth of the cellar. As it was, his view was as limited now as it had been yesterday; he could see only the steps fading into the murk of the water and the glossy water reflecting, rough, gray cement ceiling.

What was he listening for? Movement, of course. He had finally admitted it to himself: he was waiting to at least hear something move down there. If he couldn't hear it, then it would at least disturb the water with its movement.

He had spent a useless morning trying to convince himself that he was trying to make-believe something into existence; and with each box he had moved, he had become more and more sure that there was nothing fictional about the sensation he had experienced. And the one thought that kept coming back to his mind was: What

IN THE RAIN

would have happened if he hadn't been wearing waders? Would he have known for sure that it was just a bullfrog swimming in that swamp? Or just a snake?

He shuddered: anything but a snake.

The rational side of him had decided that yes, there was something down there, but it was just a natural thing. It was only when he was unpacking the dishes that the retort to that arose in his mind: why would it be anything but natural? Still, he couldn't laugh that off, couldn't ignore it. There was a tremor within him, humming like a tuning fork, that whispered there was something curious beneath the waters. The tremor moved gingerly like a fly tapping a spider's web.

Now, with his paper plate next to him in the grass, he felt the tremor more so, like an electric current, a physical hum. He remembered being seven and wondering what electricity had tasted like. His dad's saw had been plugged into an old orange snake of an extension cord, wrapped haphazardly with duct tape where the insulation had once been split. Seven years old and fresh with a science lesson in his head, he had cleverly removed the tape and lifted the cord to his mouth. Before it had touched his mouth (his dad's saw screaming around the side of the house and Lynyrd Skynyrd blasting beneath it) he could feel the current pulsating in his hand; reaching out to him. It had been a very real sensation on that sunny day—that the life running through that orange cord had wanted to be in him, wanted him to bite down. Its soft electrical hands were caressing his cheeks, drawing his gaping mouth closer.

Then, like that, he had chickened out . . . because he had heard the electric voice. An alien hum that couldn't taste good would most definitely poison him. He had left the cord in the grass, the saw still screaming, the internals uninsulated and glistening every color under the summer sky.

Now, those fingers were back. He, of course, hadn't considered the danger of electrocution yesterday, had he? Which was stupid, yes, but he still didn't think that electrocution was the problem. Electricity was still *natural*.

Lunch over and everything silent and still, he now stood and picked up the pump. He descended the stairs with the tubular box banging his thigh. He smelled of sweat and sleep, but the cellar's putrescent rot overpowered his stench; nature's deodorant, rot. When he was a step above the water, he thumbed the switch on; the pump came to life in his hand, sucking at the air and sending it through the pipe that cut across his yard and formed a creek down the back alley. The hum of the water pump, too, seemed silenced by the inaudible hum of *down here*. Not realizing he was shaking, he laid the pump in the water.

X

He slept on the couch again, but the TV was muted. The only sounds were the sweep of passing cars, and the distant thrum of the pump. Ten hours and it had pumped enough to reveal three steps; the storm drains had to be running high.

He dreamed again of the cellar. Dry. Of its open door. Of a shadow shifting across the watery floor, a shadow that wasn't right, was contorted at the right angles to make it wrong. Of stepping down the dry steps and stepping into the yellow brown light, step by hidden step, until he was standing not in the cellar but a cave of dripping colors. Stalactites of brown, dripping and pooling like wax. The yellow bulb now a cascading tear drop of yellow that never lost its form. And the black, the black beyond the cavernous edifice, was dripping and running too. It was—

IN THE RAIN

XI

He woke to rain falling heavily. The cracked window allowed him to hear the plump plats of raindrops on the cement porch. A car *whisked* past. Somewhere near, he could hear a kid chattering something incoherently on another, distant porch. The wind rustled the magnolia tree in the front yard—

The cellar. He had left the cellar door open.

For a moment, he couldn't move with the urgency he wanted. He couldn't jump off the couch; he only lay there with his arm across his eyes.

Is this how I'm going to sleep every night? With nightmares?

No, on the couch; waking up with a sore back and fragments of the late night talk shows rattling around in my head.

He sat up. The muted TV was now showing the weather, which forecasted a ninety percent chance of rain (who knows where this front came from, the weatherman laughed).

I used to fall asleep with her words in my ear: "Night, baby." And now I fall asleep to the top ten. (Do we know how long this will all last, Tom? Maria Tchecovia asked the weatherman). *Where I used to roll into her for warmth, I hug a pillow closer.*

Yeah, boss, but what about the cellar?

What about the blues? What about Miles Davis and how you saluted her as she left? What about the cellar, your place? About Mr. IQ? The mortgage? The debt? What about sleeping in the cellar on a cot? Your place. It's your place and it's flooded again.

Weakly, he rose to his feet, desperate for her; desperate to know that he could have forgiven her and she could be in the kitchen again, maybe only temporarily satisfied. But they could listen to blues, and he could tell her that it was beautiful, because it really was. He could work less. He wanted to hear the *ratta-ratta* of her laptop as she typed out one of her new poems. But for one more chance . . . geez, for one more chance, he would at least listen to it and try to like it. While a saxophone hummed in the background.

He put on the waders. And with them came more memories. The waders had been clumped at the bottom of a refrigerator box that had been filled with wadded up newspaper; the box had been wrapped in blue paper with Santa winking at no one in particular but you. And when he had opened the top of the box and continued pulling out handful after handful of newspaper, she had laughed so hard. He had covered her with the empty box, before pushing the box over.

* * * * *

It was a cold rain, and the cars that streamed past in their hissing fogs seemed dreamlike. He twirled the flashlight in his palm, a habit he had formed when he had worked as a night security guard at the Nuclear Plant when they had had their first baby-scare. He would come home at three in the morning to a house that smelled like fresh coffee; she would always be back in bed, having started him some coffee.

He looked down into the cellar. The water was lower than it had been, but the new rainwater was cascading down the steps and attempting to refill the hollow. The top of the pump, which he had inched down the last few steps and set on the floor of the cellar, was now visible; its hose ran like a fat, segmented snake out of the murky water and cut across the yard, still pumping water.

She had hated snakes. The mere mention of the "S-word" was forbidden in the house. Sometimes, a discarded towel looked too much like a snake on the bathroom floor in the middle of the night; or a drawstring that had come loose in the dryer. She would scream. She would say only that she saw an "S-word" that day. Never snake. She couldn't say it. Nor was he allowed to hiss.

In his dreams, the colors had melted. The cellar had become a cave of dissolution, of discontinuity. He had felt as though he were swimming, as though everything were swimming - everything running and filtering. What had he looked like? Had he been able

IN THE RAIN

to disconnect from himself, what would he have seen of himself? His graying hair dripping down the angle of his chin, which was dripping his tan down his chest, the hair of his chest thinning like watery ink, his feet becoming part of the floor—

The rain rivered down him, soaking his shirt. His pajamas clung to his legs. Mud seeped between his toes.

Why was he here?

Because this is my place. Mine! The cellar's murkiness looked too inviting. *The whole house was ours. It always would be.*

Something splashed out of his shielded vision, and he felt something ignite inside of himself. There was something down there that was *beyond* him. *Beyond* a bullfrog or a fish. Beyond a snake. Beyond. Simply beyond. And on some level, he had known it. Like a man anxious to discover a hidden trove, he had anticipated that whatever lurked through the murk of the water had been something that shouldn't be. The concentric circles from whatever had caused the splash now became a tide licking at the steps.

The rain fell and sighed. And the pump hummed.

And he wept.

Suddenly, he was lonely. Tired. The rain sighed. The pump hummed. The hose jittered between his feet like a nervous cymbal. He thought of the blues, of the accurate melancholy that comforted him; he also found something comforting in this hollowed foundation beneath his house. Whatever thing was in there, he was sure that it was calling out to him.

He descended the steps, his face slick with the sheen of tears or rain. Before his toes touched the dark water, he hesitated, his voice caught in his throat. It was so dark.

But it's my place. Mine. She never saw this. And he was right. It was his.

The water closed around his ankle. And immediately, he sensed something approaching, like a spider alerted that some fly has tripped its web. Something beyond and unreal, that understood what it was like to simply exist. He felt its warmth emanate toward him and understood that this was just a fragment of its cyclopean shape.

Standing like a man in a cathedral, he leaned down and reverently flicked the pump off. The hum died instantly.

The rising water licked at his shins, at his knees. In a matter of seconds, it was at his waist again. And whatever it was in the water, it\s warmth kept curling against him. The water, so warm now, pooled around his stomach. A chortling voice reverberated through his mind and bones, resonating mostly in his spine.

He thought of the electric current he had once felt reaching out for his face; he thought of Anne, of how she smiled differently, of how she smelled differently; he thought of their house above him, how she would be in every corner even though her stuff was over ten miles away; he thought of the solitude that rain can bring.

The water eased over his shoulders.

Something splashed in the far corner, a spray of something dark.

Bad. It's bad, he thought, but he no longer cared. It was too late. The water touched his chin, and he stood there.

Another splash: an arc of radiant colors that seemed to glimmer in the grayness.

It's a celebration, he thought. And the electric buzz pulsed in him again because, he sensed, he was right.

The water continued to rise.

The water rose above his eyes, but he didn't shut them. And then he saw the colors begin to run, every defined shape wavering and losing its form. The lines of reality seemed to lace with one another.

Something colorful roiled in the water. He could see it rolling in the murk of the cellar, a shapeless mass like oil but moving with intelligence and intent—

It came for him, fully now, its geometry distorting and reengaging itself as it drew nearer.

IN THE RAIN

And then the water was still.

XII

She shouldn't have been playing in the rain, she knew that, but mommy was gone to the store, and what mommy didn't know wouldn't hurt her. Lilly jumped in another puddle barefooted, the mud squishing up between her toes. She laughed and aimed for the next puddle, the next plot in her game of water-hopscotch—

She landed with another splash that speckled her pale legs with dark freckles.

The rain cascaded over her.

She jumped again and landed with a splash. Brown water arced into the air.

Then, she saw the end: the stream behind her house. It had risen with the rain (and Jackson's drainage, though she didn't know that he even existed) and raced steadily along now. A mischievous grin crossed her face.

She could cannonball into it. It would be cold, would be freezing. Mommy would be so mad, probably, but she could run in and change real fast, couldn't she?

She leapt and landed in the waist-high creek. A scream escaped her. It was much colder than she expected but—

Something tapped her leg, twice.

Ricky Massengale lives with his wife and son in Russellville, AR. His work has appeared in Nebo, RE:AL, Everyday Poets, EarthSpeak, Full Armor, Pond Ripples Magazine, and the anthology Daily Flash: 365 Days of Flash Fiction. In 2006, a small press published a chapbook of his experimental poetry. He looks for beauty in broken things.

Francis
Georgina Morales

FRANCIS REYNOLDS WAS AN OBESE MAN; he was forty years old and had no friends at all. His bad temper had always alienated people around him. From very early on in his life, all Francis could remember were words of hate and unkindness. His parents could barely take care of themselves; with odd jobs here and there and his father's growing addiction to gambling, they were too busy to really care. When Francis was eight years old his mother was diagnosed with schizophrenia and her mean vain took a life of its own.

Food had been his only solace; Francis' neighbor, Ms. Moreti, came everyday to help his mother and take care of him. She was of Italian descent and made the most wonderful lasagna he had ever tasted, all while singing and dancing to her own tunes. Those were the only times when happy voices filled the house and the sense of tension was lifted. A few years later, Ms. Moreti eloped with her latest boyfriend; rumors ran wild to the fact that they had settled in New Haven looking for some excitement. Whatever the truth, all that mattered was that she had left and never looked back, leaving Francis filled with hatred but with a lasting love for pasta.

Francis hated the human race and felt the blind conviction that it hated him back. Over time, he developed his own obsessions. Completely isolated from society, he hadn't set a foot out of his parents' house in ten years. The last time he had gone into the streets was to attend his father's funeral; after that he inherited the house and stopped any communication with others except for a weekly call to Mark Johnston's King Supermarket to get his groceries.

FRANCIS

With the increase in popularity and variety of products available through the Internet, Francis had become a shopaholic and a hoarder. For years he indulged himself in his three passions: shopping, eating and collecting. His habits got so out of hand that eventually his neighbors called the Sheriff into action when the most horrific smell leaked out of the house making them believe their unseen neighbor had died.

"Francis, we have no other option. You need to comply or the City will be forced to deem the house a health risk and therefore, inhabitable." Said Jonathan Meyers, Saybrook's Deputy, trying to reason with the obnoxious man.

"So, in order to keep my house I have to allow some self-righteous dirt bag into my home to judge my lifestyle and conclude what I can keep and what I can't? This is outrageous! If I died in there of a heart attack and rats ate my remains NOBODY would give a damn... as long as the neighbors don't complain!!" Francis yelled in anger hoping the entire block could hear him. He closed the door with all his might.

"I'm sorry Francis but this isn't over. I'll come back in a week and I expect to smell the difference!"

The bitter forty-year-old felt a bit disappointed when the door didn't hit Meyers. He was an intelligent man and knew that when Tom Harden, the Sheriff, came by closing the door wasn't going to do much to solve his problems.

He paid attention to the inside of the house; it was impossible to see the hardwood floors underneath discarded papers, old boxes, and garbage in general. Francis couldn't smell the hideousness but only God knew how many dead things were lurking under all that stuff, let alone the fauna growing inside his refrigerator cramped full with moldy food.

After thinking for a couple of days he concluded that he needed to buy more time. The moment he had been waiting for, for a long time was close; time for retribution, but in the meantime he didn't want those people inside his house.

In a small city like Saybrook, most people knew each other and that offered options to deal with his situation that would simply not be possible in a big city. Francis intended to take full advantage of such options. He called for a meeting with the Sheriff; his plan meant taking a big risk but Harden was a predictable creature and that gave him an edge.

Tom Harden was a prime example of small-town-mentality. He had lived in Hartford during his college years but after that he had come back to never leave again. He became very private and weary of people, mostly newcomers. Harden had gone to great extremes to keep his secret out of the gossip mill but speculations were rampant; something had happened to him in the city and everyone had a theory. The stories went from love at first sight that ended in heartbreak to wild parties with spiked drinks and drug addictions; however, there was one that was particularly outlandish.

Jennifer Royster was the local medium and, for the most part, helped women with candles and prayers for love and money; in Harden's mind she was a witch. She claimed it all had been revealed to her in a dream. In it, she'd seen Tom being fooled into producing biological weapons for some shady characters. Royster believed karma would come back to hunt the now Sheriff, dragging everyone close to him to hell. Since he had came back to Saybrook, she decided to pass her knowledge along to her clients but considering where the information was coming from, more often than not it was considered nonsense.

Some years had gone by, Harden had been elected Sheriff, and rumors had died down; the new big talk of town was Francis Reynolds.

The meeting had been a closed affair; only Francis, Jonathan, and Tom were present. The City, by means of its Sheriff, exposed the rules and possible punishment if they weren't followed; Reynolds, on the other hand, defended himself.

FRANCIS

"Look, you have no right to rummage through my house and throw away stuff that isn't hurting anyone. These are my things and there's a reason why I need them; a very important reason."

Francis was trying to keep his tone even, but not making it. He was wearing a t-shirt that had been pink at some point but years of wear and tear had left it faded and thin as onionskin. His skin was pale to the point of transparency and he was so fat that every movement left him gasping for air.

Meyers looked at him with aversion; Francis' disgruntled appearance and wild eyes were a far cry from the kid he once knew. They had attended school together. Back then, Jonathan was an average kid, not particularly popular but not bullied like Francis. Jonathan always felt disgust for the overweight teen; in his eyes Reynolds' shy demeanor was a sign of weakness that made him a beacon for the predators of the school. *"If you don't defend yourself, then you deserve the things that happen to you."* Jonathan told Francis once in third grade; after that they never spoke again. In high school Meyers played sports and bullied 'the fat kid with the girly name' like all the others.

"And what is that reason?" asked the Deputy in a skeptical tone.

Francis' reaction to the acid comment was fast and unexpected; the kid that couldn't do anything to help himself was now an adult full of rage. With agility impossible for his immense body, the infuriated man spun in Jonathan's direction with such violence that the Sheriff jumped up from his seat behind the desk and Jonathan moved a step back.

"That's right." Tom intervened. He was trying to call Francis' attention before his monolithic weight crushed his Deputy, now with his back to the door. "Maybe if you explain it to us, we could find some middle ground"

The huge forty-year-old never lifted his gaze from Meyers' eyes. He was enjoying the effect he had on the uniformed man backing up against the door that seemed about to run. Adrenaline rushed through Francis' veins and for a moment he understood why bullies came back for more; it was like a drug.

A shy knock on the crystal door broke the tension and made the three men jump. It was the secretary, Tanya, with a cup of coffee.

When Tanya closed the door behind her, the talk reassumed, but in a lighter way. Francis concentrated on his plan and Meyers made sure to speak as little as possible, although some of the things being said were completely outrageous.

Francis Reynolds proceeded to explain he had trust worthy information of a terrorist cell planning an attack on the USA and how their first target would be the quiet small town of Saybrook.

The Sheriff and his Deputy looked at each other in utter awe. The only question Tom managed to ask was for the name of the contact or how he had gotten access to such sensible matters; to which an even crazier explanation followed.

"I met him through the net." continued Francis, "I subscribed to a magazine about Government mess-ups and covert operations. Curiosity won me over and I broke my rule of no contact with others; I logged into a discussion panel and met Robert there. After that we've been secretly communicating; he's extremely intelligent and loves lasagna."

"So, Robert, is it?" said Tom trying to find any thread of logic in this mess. "Robert is a terrorist?" He was now pacing behind his desk with his hands in his head.

In answer, the obese man nodded, he was clearly uncomfortable talking about this. He was sweating like a criminal about to break. Jonathan just sat there next to him, without a clue as to where this was going.

"Fine, for the sake of argument let's say I believe you; but you have to explain me - why would they want to attack Saybrook? There's nothing here! And what does this have to do with your house being a health risk?" completed Harden, now showing clear signs of irritation.

FRANCIS

"First, I've been preparing for the attack and that stuff in my house is what I need to survive when it happens. They'll do it here because we're so close to big cities, yet so far that it'll take them too long to contain it in the town. Think about it: New Haven, Boston, New York! Don't you see it? It'll be some sort of powder that'll cause sickness and before somebody gets to Saybrook... it's going to be too late" Francis had stood up carried away by his excitement; he also had a twisted look in his face. When everything was over he would stand victorious over his tormentors.

The Sheriff was furious. It was clear that this parasite was talking about biological warfare; the witch was probably in on the joke. This sloth had come right into his office to mock him; it was too much to take.

We'll see who laughs at last... You don't poke fun at Thomas Harden and expect no retaliation.

"You've gone too far Reynolds. I won't allow you to ridicule the authority." His blue eyes seemed made of ice and with each sentence Francis felt like a slap was delivered to his face. "You have the rest of the week to do the best you can. On Monday 15th another inspection will take place and the City will finish the cleaning if necessary. Now, get out of here"

Francis left the place humiliated. When he got to his house, he would have closed the door with bricks and mortar had he had some lying around.

I told them everything; I gave them a chance to save themselves but they'll pay for their stubbornness!

Of course he hadn't told them everything. He didn't tell them he had proposed the town as the target, or the fact that Robert was a code name; but he had said enough to jeopardize the attack. If any of those two scumbags were to ring the alarm, it might cause problems. The reason why he had gone forth anyway was that he knew them and he knew they wouldn't believe him; what he wasn't expecting was the Sheriff's reaction. The ruse hadn't won him much time.

A soft blipping came from his room; it was the computer informing him of an email. He recognized the address.

Robert!

Francis didn't know Robert's real name but he understood; if you're a terrorist you can't go about your life telling everybody.

His chubby hand took the mouse and clicked to open it.

THE PRESENT IS ON ITS WAY; IT'LL BE THERE WITHIN A WEEK. BE PREPARED.

It was shorter than other communications from his contact, but the message was clear. Francis was ecstatic. Still, he'd have to do something to buy some time and avoid that stupid Harden from throwing away his things. They were about to see who was right and Francis would be very happy to close his door on the noses of the dying townspeople who had shunned him.

The following week everybody in Saybrook talked about how much movement there was in the Reynolds household. After years of wondering if there was still someone alive inside, for days now many neighbors had seen Francis coming in and out of the place; he had his front yard covered with black garbage bags and it had taken the recollection truck several hours to get it out of site. The smells invading the streets were maddening, going from rotten chicken to dead squirrels.

Giving the townsfolk more reason for speculation was the amount of people bringing new stuff into the house. At least as much as he had gotten out, Francis had bought anew; but the most unexpected thing came with the closing of the week. The Reynolds kid had brought an ironworker from the outskirts of town and let him inside his house for the better part of the day. Nobody had set a foot inside since his drunken father's wake.

FRANCIS

The day of the inspection the town was ablaze of gossip. Tom asked Jonathan to do the inspection himself; he knocked on the decrepit door at ten in the morning with an overwhelming sense of dread.

"Good morning officer," greeted Francis with open disdain.

"Good morning Francis. I'm here to check on things. How's everything going?" The Deputy tried to be optimistic but he knew it was going to be a hard day when he caught a glimpse of the hallway behind the unruly white male.

"I cleaned everything. Do you really need to come in?" Francis wasn't trying to be impolite; he just didn't like Meyers but he knew that until the first symptom of the attack presented itself, he was at the mercy of Tom Harden. Reluctant, he got out of the way to let the tall blond man in uniform get in.

Jonathan opened his eyes in surprise as he saw how that big man in gray sweatpants squeezed himself to get through that hallway. The right wall was covered by dozens of boxes from ceiling to floor, making the already small space really tight. Francis' old Mickey Mouse t-shirt made a ripping sound when it got stuck in the protruding end of one of the packages, but he had no reaction and continued like nothing had happened. When he got to the other side of the barricade he turned and waited for Jonathan to follow.

Meyers moved towards that ridiculous Mickey Mouse t-shirt with less effort. He kept his eyes on the other man's face, looking for any sign of the person he once knew.

Francis' father, Bruce, had been a handsome man before his addictions ruined his life; he was known as quite the lady's man with suave ways and warm green eyes. Now Jonathan could barely see the resemblance; the son's face was scarred by acne and had morphed into a mask contorted by loathing.

The Deputy proceeded to walk around the main floor, basement, and bedrooms upstairs. After two hours he reached a decision.

"Francis, this is not enough. I appreciate how you've removed everything that was thrown on the floor, but there's pilling boxes everywhere; you can hardly move throughout the rooms!" He was as polite as possible; he didn't want to infuriate him when there was no one to come to his aid.

"But there's no smell anymore!" Francis pouted.

"I know but..." An intermittent signal on his walkie-talkie interrupted him. He took it off his belt and answered.

"Yes, Tom. This is Jonathan"

First there was some static but a couple of seconds later they heard Tom's voice.

"How's everything going out there?" His voice came a bit electronic.

"Not ready, yet. There are still a lot of boxes" Jonathan sneaked a look to check on Reynolds' response.

"Ok. Do what you have to do; I want that out of our hair today. Tomorrow is the Concert and I don't have time to deal with that." The stiff voice was upset.

"I got it." The Deputy turned back to Francis and went on, "Ok. Let's make this right; I can help you move boxes from one place to the other in order to open more space for movement. You can organize everything that's out of boxes later."

Jonathan felt uneasy, the foreboding feeling was getting stronger and he wanted to get out of there soon.

Francis took the opportunity; as long as this man didn't throw out anything, he could let it go. Judging from the Sheriff's tone, by tomorrow this would be over; he was happy.

They worked hard. Jonathan had no idea what was in those boxes but they were heavy. Three hours later, he decided to take a brake and went into the kitchen to get water. The countertops were littered with meat drying in salt; every available corner was covered with gallons of bottle water. He opened three different cupboards looking for a glass but all he found were cans of food.

FRANCIS

What is this man doing? He has food for a battalion! On the other hand, how much does he weigh?

A very distressed Francis interrupted his train of thought.

"What are you doing? These are my things!" He was covered in sweat and exhausted but he closed the cupboard doors so fast that Jonathan was stunned again by his outburst of agility.

"I'm thirsty; I was looking for a glass," said Meyers in a tone that implied an apology. "What are you planning to do with all this food? And what is it with all those iron doors and windows, anyway?"

He pointed to an iron protection, designed to cover the whole window when closed. There were similar contraptions on every window and door; it was like a fortress.

"I told you, there will be an attack on this town and I'm prepared to survive it," answered Reynolds with a matter-of-fact attitude. He took a glass from a nearby box and filled it with tap water; he handed it to the other man who clearly was at a loss for a rebuke. A new call from his walkie-talkie put an end to the discussion.

"Yes, Tom. I'm here" Jonathan kept staring at the fat man, still thinking of an answer to his crazy statement.

"There's something strange going on today. I don't know what's in the water but people seem to be very violent; we've been breaking fights all over the city. When are you finishing?"

"There's a lot more to do but I could leave Reynolds to do it by himself and come back later for a check." Jonathan was concerned; it wasn't like Tom to hurry him on an official matter.

"It's ok. Just finish today. If I need you I'll call you back." Tom was obviously tired.

Goosebumps covered Jonathan's skin when he saw the sardonic smile on Francis' face. He really wanted to get out of the house.

"C'mon, let's finish with this already" Said the officer while moving towards the hallway once again; the owner of the house followed him. The glass of water was left behind, untouched.

The clock marked six-thirty when the last call came in. This time Harden was desperate, the violence had escalated and there was a riot in Mercy Hospital. The hospital was merely a block from Francis' home. Both men came out, one trying to help, the other wanting to witness the end.

When they got to the corner of Hollow's End and King's Rd., they saw three patrol cars in the middle of the intersection, forming a barricade to protect the officers and those who had been able to escape. Bloodied people ran in every direction and there were screams and gunfire.

"That's Sharon Hayward!" said Jonathan when he saw, in shock, Tom shooting her in the head.

"I know! We all know these people, but they're not themselves anymore. Sharon was killed an hour ago in a brawl." Tom's usual calmness was replaced by an abrasive tone. He had no time to explain. "Just take your gun and shoot to the head."

"What?" The Deputy was perplexed. It couldn't be. He spun and locked eyes with Francis, who was laughing in hysterical fits and moving backwards.

Andrew Rutger grabbed Reynolds from behind trying to hold him in a deadly embrace but his overweight made it impossible. Francis elbowed him and ran. Rutger recovered and kept moving, this time toward Tom and Jonathan.

Meyers was petrified; Andrew and he played softball every Thursday night but he looked different. There was something hideous in his friend's movements, unnatural. He was hauling his right leg turned in an unnatural angle from the knee down; deep red stains were evident on his clothing. Right under his right knee the linen fabric had a rip and with growing anxiety Jonathan spotted a white branch-like flange; it was the broken bone.

FRANCIS

Soon after his ghastly discovery, Jonathan saw Tanya; the secretary was coming from the other side of the road. Her face was mauled, her left cheek hanging from her jaw line; she was very pale and her arms were bitten too. A creeping thought plagued him; *they are DEAD!*

He looked around hastily. In the far left corner of King's road he could see sixteen-year-old Anna Marie being attacked by her mom and dad. People on the street were running fast while others screeched. The smell of gunpowder and blood was overpowering as was the cacophony of gunshots and screams; but the worst of all the sounds came from the monsters.

THEY SPEAK was the last coherent thought of Jonathan's mind. His eyes grew abnormally big, demented and void of reason as he heard the lifeless wretches go over their unnerving chant.

"Huungry, huuunngry, huu…" They gargled and dragged their depraved bodies in an unending freak show.

Tanya came closer to Tom, who was too busy killing the demons in front of him to pay attention to his back. With a bloodcurdling scream he fell to the ground. All Jonathan could see of the once beautiful woman was the piece of meat dangling from her face while she made Tom's neck her dinner.

In blind terror he ran past Andrew, who tried to catch him with a sluggish movement but failed. He ran as fast as he could but when he reached Francis, he was closing his door. Something bit his right calf and soon after a sharp pain on his Achilles tendon followed; they had gotten to him. The last thing his eyes saw, were Francis' mocking green eyes and his horrible smile with no soul. He pounded on the door, but all he could hear was the heavy noise of metal closing.

Born in Mexico City, Georgina has also lived in Spain, Canada, and the US. Georgina is compelled to horror stories and everything that goes bump in the night, even if it terrifies her. In an attempt to understand her fear, she writes about it.

HAND OUT
Matt Kurtz

HIS HEAD THROBBED. HIS THROAT WAS DRY. He was cold; so very cold. He lay in the ditch on the side of the deserted road with wet leaves stuck to his face. Paralyzed - only able to stare at the bare tree branches that loomed into the sky. Dear God. He had been so careless, making the biggest mistake of his soon-to-be shortened life.

* * * * *

Only an hour earlier, Mark had pulled his car into the parking lot of the electronics store on that cold Sunday afternoon. There was a DVD player that was on sale and since his was on the fritz, he decided to pick up a new one. He hoped the model was on a palette of boxes in the walkway so he could grab it and avoid any salespeople. He hated it when the stores didn't have the boxed items directly under the display models; that meant that you had to deal with a salesperson and ask them to get you one from the back. That also meant that you had to listen to all their sales talk of how *'this model right over here is a little more pricier but does so much more.'* But knowing that they also had to make a living, Mark would politely listen to their spiels until they were done and then say that he could only afford the model on sale. After that, they wouldn't give him the time of day—which is exactly the way Mark liked it, since he preferred to keep his distance from people.

As his car pulled into a spot, he saw a man and woman loading multiple shopping bags under the raised hatch of their SUV and hoped they had left a player for him.

HAND OUT

He also saw a man walking between the cars, approaching the couple as they slammed the hatchback shut and made their way to the front of the vehicle.

The man didn't look homeless, but he definitely looked down on his luck. He wore a long dark overcoat and a knit skull cap that was too tight for his large, potato-shaped head. The cap squished his face down, causing it to wrinkle up like a Shar-Pei dog. His gruff face, large build, and beady eyes (that shifted back and forth under a thick unibrow, horribly accented even more by the tight cap) made him quite intimidating. Even though Mark watched from a distance within the comfort of his warm, locked car, he still found himself sinking lower into the seat to escape detection.

He saw the man ask the couple something to which they politely shrugged and shook their heads. The man watched them get into their SUV, then turned and looked around the parking lot.

Mark sunk a little lower, holding his breath.

The man spotted another set of shoppers leaving the store and made his way toward them. Mark knew it was only moments before it was his turn to be accosted.

He glanced down at the sales flier sitting on the seat beside him and wondered if he *really* needed to save a few bucks on the player. Maybe he should go to another store location? But the closest one was across city lines. The money he'd save on the sale would only be used on the gas to drive all that way. As he debated whether it was worth it, he glanced in his rearview mirror and saw the exhaust from his tailpipe billowing up into the cold air. It was acting like a smoke signal that might send the man in Mark's direction.

Mark quickly fumbled with the keys, shutting off the engine. He checked to see if the guy had spotted him. He didn't (and thank God for that); instead the man was watching the entrance of the store, waiting for the next set of customers to exit.

Mark knew the guy's type. He'd been approached by enough of them—asking with a hand out, a false look of humility in their eyes, and the same damn sob story spewing from their mouth. He imagined that there must be some secret seminar that they attended; one where they gathered, compared stories that reaped the maximum donations, and coached one another on how to spot the best schmucks to approach.

Mark, whatever his type was, seemed to be their Number One Schmuck. He'd lost count of the number of times he'd been approached. Even though he made every conscious effort to stay inconspicuous, they always picked him out of a crowd. He'd see them approaching out of the corner of his eye and hope they would just move past him. But they never did. Just as he'd reach the sanctuary that was his car, he'd hear a voice directly over his shoulder. "Excuse me, sir?" Instinctively, he'd freeze, thinking that someone had finally discovered his secret. Slowly turning around, he'd see the forced look of modesty on their face as they stood there, staring at him. "Um…my car ran out of gas and I'm short on cash. Do you think you could spare a few bucks to help me out?" Mark wanted to ask to see their car keys to verify the existence of said car…but always wound up giving them a few dollars instead.

Then there was the time that Mark was thrown for a loop while washing his car. With every bin full of people soaping up and hosing down their vehicles, this guy wanders out from nowhere, and of course, makes a direct bee-line to Mark. "Excuse me, sir? I'll help you wash your car if you give me a couple bucks for doing so." At least this one was offering a service in exchange for compensation. But Mark didn't want his help because then they'd have to converse while they washed his car. What if Mark let something slip? Or the man got too close and saw that something was slightly off with Mark? When he offered to just give the man a few bucks without the need of his help, the man's friendly demeanor became confrontational. "I ain't asking for a handout, man. I ain't no beggar! I told ya I'd help ya, if ya pay me for it!" Mark started to shake, partly out of fear and partly from

HAND OUT

what he knew was trying to force its way to the surface. That white-hot pain behind his eyes always started when he got too excited, like some warped defense mechanism. When it came, the safest place for *everyone* was for him to be at home alone. Luckily, the man stormed off to preserve his pride and the teeth in Mark's mouth. When he watched the man disappear around the corner, Mark bolted, rushing home with the soapy rinse still covering his car. Later, when he was alone in the dark and able to control the burning in his brain, Mark couldn't help but wonder what might've happened if he hadn't made it home in time? What if he lost control of *it*? Well, if that were to happen, the world would definitely find out what he—

KNOCK! KNOCK! KNOCK! The rap on his window caused Mark to jump so high he almost slammed his head into the car's roof.

The Shar-Pei-faced man stood just outside his door, motioning for him to roll down the window. Mark took a deep breath and lowered it.

"Hey, man. I was wondering if you could help me out?"

Mark cleared his throat and tried to put on an air of casualness. "Sure, what's up?" Any nonchalance went out the window when his voice cracked on the last word.

"Listen, my car broke down and I was wondering if you could give me a ride to a friend's house?"

Mark felt his stomach wrap completely around his spine. He was fully prepared with a response if the man only wanted cash, telling him that he only carried plastic. But this—this totally threw him for a loop! "Ahh...actually I...I was kinda in a hurry..." was all he could muster up.

The man let off a disbelieving shrug. "Then what are ya doing just sittin' here with the engine off?"

"I mean...I was just about to go into the store to pick something up."

"Hey, I ain't going nowhere, I can wait 'til ya come out. No biggie."

"Well, ah...actually...do you want to use my cell and call your friend to come get you?"

"I would've already done that but he ain't got no phone."

Mark knew he was trapped. The man noticed his uneasiness.

"Listen, buddy. I'm just a guy that's shit outta luck and needs a ride. I feel bad enough as it is."

"Well...ah...where does your friend live?" Maybe it was in another city or something. He could tell the guy that he had an appointment in the complete opposite direction.

The man pointed over his shoulder. "Just a few exits up." He looked at his watch. "I'd walk but he leaves to go to work in about a half hour and even if I ran the whole way, I'd never make it there before then. And if I miss him, I'm really screwed."

Mark sat there, unable to come up with an excuse and too scared to just say no. He watched an endless parade of shoppers exiting the store, all getting safely into their cars without a single hassle. He wanted to point them out to the man. Why not ask them? Why me?! His eyes shifted back and forth between the people, hoping the man beside his door would stop to see what he was looking at, realize that there were other fish out there, and throw this little guppy that was wasting his time back into the water.

"Please, sir. I wouldn't be asking if I really didn't need the help."

Mark knew it could be the biggest mistake of his life, but nodded anyway. "Okay, hop in."

As the man walked around to the other side of the car, Mark fought to take a deep breath.

The man jiggled the handle and it took a moment for Mark to reach for the button to automatically unlock the door. This was his last chance. He could start the car, slam it in reverse, and peel out of there. The man smiled through the passenger window and

HAND OUT

pointed that the door was locked. Mark hesitated for another moment. *No, don't do it. You're going to regret it*, echoed a tiny voice in his mind. But the voice was quickly silenced when his index finger shot forward, pushing against the button. The lock popped up. It was too late now. What was done was done.

The man climbed in and plopped down in the passenger seat. After slamming the door, he extended his hand to Mark. "My name's Johnny, by the way."

Mark shook it limply. "Mark. Good to meet you Johnny."

Johnny rubbed his hands together to get the blood flowing again. "Man, is it cold out there!"

Mark started the car and shifted one of the heater vents in Johnny's direction. Johnny smiled at the gesture.

The car stopped at the entrance to the parking lot and Mark gripped the wheel tightly. "So which way?"

"Just make a left and get on the highway going south."

Mark flipped on his blinker, checked in both directions, rechecked, and then made the turn.

As Mark drove down the road, Johnny leaned his head back and closed his eyes. "Ya know, not a lot of people will give a stranger a ride nowadays."

Mark forced a smile and shrugged, even though his passenger couldn't see it. "Not a problem."

"To some people it is. Glad you're not one of them, ya know?"

They drove in silence, exactly the way Mark hoped it would be. But then Johnny took a deep breath and sprung back to life, his eyes shooting open. "So, tell me Mark. You married?"

"No," he said, hoping that was the end of it.

"Yeah, me neither." Johnny stared ahead for a moment then turned to face Mark. "Live alone?"

Mark didn't want to answer. He wasn't accustomed to giving such personal information, but he did it anyway to prevent the situation from getting awkward. "Yes."

Johnny nodded, "Me, too."

There was nothing more for a good minute. Mark was grateful for the silence. Then his stomach twitched a little when he saw, from the corner of his eye, that Johnny stuck his right hand into the inside breast pocket of his overcoat.

"Ya know, Mark? The only thing that sucks about livin' alone is what if somethin' happens to us? There's no one there to report it, ya know?"

Mark felt his stomach loop a second lap around his spine.

"I mean, let's say that we're sittin' at home and our ticker gives out. Who the hell is gonna know that we went to Grandma's farm and all?"

Mark could only shrug.

Johnny moved his hand around under his coat. "Guess the landlord would, after he starts getting complaints about the smell from our neighbors, huh?"

Mark compressed the brake and the car slowed to a stop. Johnny looked ahead, saw the traffic jam at the red light, then glanced at his watch.

Mark *knew* he shouldn't have gone this way because of the mall traffic. Now he was stuck with this Johnny guy for even longer. He tried to take a deep breath to calm himself before the throbbing at his temples had a chance to start.

But it was too late. Like an airplane approaching in the distance, the rumbling working its way to his brain only grew louder. *Please...NOT NOW!*

"Well, this sucks," Johnny said indifferently as he glanced ahead at the traffic. Then he turned back to Mark. "Anyways, like I was saying—"

Please, stop! Don't do this!

"What if...say...we just never came home one day? Just vanished into thin air, ya know?"

Mark had to get this guy out of his car. *Now.*

HAND OUT

"...Maybe an alien abduction or somethin'...or some crazy person."

Vibrations of fear worked their way out of Mark's chest, traveled down his arms, and filled his fingertips. He clutched the steering wheel tight so as to not give it away that he was shaking.

"Who the hell would report us missin' and all?" Johnny asked.

Mark saw an opening to the right. Beyond it was a side road where he could turn off the busy street and get the hell out of this jam—the one outside the car, but mostly from the one in it.

Johnny continued. "I mean, who's to say that—"

Mark whipped the car over so fast that Johnny braced himself against the dash with his free hand, yet kept the other one still concealed in his jacket. "Whoa, man! You drive for NASCAR or somethin'?" Johnny sputtered, clearly caught off-guard by the sudden movement.

Mark's car stopped only a few feet from where he could make the turn onto the side street. He inched the car forward, stopping only millimeters from the bumper in front of him. *C'mon! C'mon! C'MON!*

Johnny smiled, pointing back to the left lane. "We really should be over there if you wanna go southbound on the highway."

Mark didn't respond. He couldn't even hear his passenger speak over the pounding in his head.

The vehicle in front of them moved an inch forward—just enough for Mark to make the turn. As the car whipped around the corner, the back passenger tire clipped the curb and both men bounced with the vehicle. Mark saw that Johnny refused to remove his right hand, still buried within his jacket.

"Where are you goin', man? Ya know a back way or somethin'?"

Mark nodded and sped up. The car roared down the deserted road. He refused to let this happen. For Christ's sake, all he wanted was a DVD player. That was why he left the house this morning. That was all that was supposed to happen today! Not this!! Not now!! He had to get this creep out of his car before it was too late!!!

"Ya might slow down a bit. I don't want ya gettin' pulled over on account of me and all. We'll make it in time, if ya just loop back around."

Mark could feel the nausea rising in a wave over the knots in his stomach. He slammed his foot on the brake, sending the car into a skid across the wet leaves.

"Jesus Christ, man!" Johnny's squeal was almost as high-pitched as that of the tires.

When the car slid to a stop, he looked over at Mark, who was staring at him with eyes on fire.

"Get out!" Mark yelled. "Get out, now!!"

Johnny sat there in shock. "What...dude? What's your problem?"

"Get out, goddamn it!!"

Johnny looked around at the deserted woods. "Here? What the fuck, man?"

"GET OUT..." Mark screamed. He closed his eyes as his head slammed deep into the headrest. "...while you still can." The last few words were growled out in a voice much deeper than his own.

The hair prickled under Johnny's skull cap from the drastic change in the dude's voice. Still keeping his hand buried in his pocket, Johnny silently watched him.

When Mark finally opened his eyes, he suddenly looked a hell of a lot calmer. Johnny waited a moment and then pulled out the pack of cigarettes from inside the breast pocket of his overcoat. He extended them to Mark with a trembling hand. "Here, man. Ya want a cigarette? It'll help calm ya down and all," he whispered delicately.

Mark stared at him, completely ignoring the good gesture of the smoke. "You never finished what you were saying," Mark

HAND OUT

growled. "About us living alone and disappearing. What was that really all about?"

Johnny looked lost; the extreme change in the dude's voice was really throwing him for a loop. It was like he was possessed or something. "Ah...just that, I don't know...maybe being married...ya, know... having an old lady that's waitin' on ya at home wouldn't be so bad. Right?"

A smile crept onto Mark's face. "No, Johnny. You and I were meant to be alone in this world. Because how else would I get away with what I'm about to do to you?"

Before Johnny could ask a question that ended with "man", "ya know?", or "and all", Mark's lids stretched wide open and his eyes rolled back in his head. What stared back from his glistening sockets were basically two, huge polished cue balls. Mark let out a deafening wail as his jaw cracked and seemed to dislocate from his skull, widening almost down to his chest.

Johnny scrambled for the door handle, wrapped his hands around it, and yanked hard. But the door was locked. He frantically dug in his side pocket and pulled something out. When he whirled back to the driver's seat with the object raised all he saw was the ghastly face and the enormous mouth lined with razor-sharp teeth.

It lunged at him and all went black.

* * * * *

When Johnny woke on the side of the road, he was wet and cold, his body shivering uncontrollably. His throat was incredibly dry, making it impossible to swallow. He dropped the switchblade that he was clutching—never getting a chance to flip it open—and slowly raised his hand to rub his throat, feeling his fingers sink deep into the gaping hole in his neck.

As he laid there bleeding out, his final thought was one of regret. Not that he shouldn't have asked the stranger for a ride, but that he should've just risked robbing the schmuck back in the store's parking lot instead of playing some cat and mouse bullshit game, waiting until they pulled up in front of the vacant house—where there would be no witnesses.

Matt Kurtz

Matt Kurtz writes in his spare time when not working at a small advertising company in Texas. His fiction has appeared in numerous anthologies.

FILE 8962: FOUND IN APARTMENT 211 ON CLEAN-UP DAY 2
Tiffany E. Wilson

BEFORE THE OUTBREAK I DIDN'T HAVE A CHANCE. Obviously, this isn't what I had in mind when I pictured us together. Who dreams of keeping the love of their life tied to a folding chair? It's not like I had any other choice.

I first met Cathy outside the basement laundry room. I wouldn't call it "love at first sight" but I was instantly slain by her silky blonde hair, luscious curves, and blue eyes clearer than tap water.

A lacy pink thong tumbled out of her basket as she passed. I froze at first, but then felt silly just staring at it like that, so I grabbed it and said, "Oh, your...uh...this."

As she walked toward me I knew this was it, the moment she'd fall deeply in love with me.

She tossed the underwear in her basket. "Thanks." That was it.

For the past two years, I've kept an eye on her. I figured out her name from the Victoria's Secret catalogs in the recycling bin. Eventually I met her boyfriend—well, I saw him. He was around a lot and I guessed they were living together. He looked like a mess, like all he cared about was being successful and working out and traveling to awesome places to do awesome things. Total loser. Cathy called him Tiger when they had sex. I just assumed that was his name.

Everything changed on the second day of the outbreak. The national disaster wasn't declared yet, but the office I temped at closed for the day. To avoid the chaos and infectants outside, I

FILE 8962: FOUND IN APARTMENT 211

locked my door and watched the news: shaky cell phone footage and hypothesizing scientists talking in circles.

During a commercial break I noticed a thudding noise coming from the hall. Through the peephole I saw the back of a woman who kept shuffling forward and banging her forehead against the opposite door over and over.

I opened my door for a better look. "Cathy?"

Her body turned slowly with a low guttural moan.

In one glance I diagnosed the symptoms: pale, purple skin, trance like state, and lack of discernible vocal communication. There was a moment of recognition, but then she lunged, openmouthed, roaring like a velociraptor.

I grabbed my souvenir didgeridoo from its stand near the door and smacked her upside the head. Don't get me wrong, I'm all about feminism and not hitting girls, but she was coming at me and it was probably self-defense.

When Cathy hit the ground, I freaked out. The news said infectants were best subdued with head wounds and I was pretty sure I killed her. She wasn't looking too healthy either—there was a nasty oozing wound on her shoulder and her arm kinda looked like it was decaying. As I leaned closer, she started twitching and pretty soon she was on her feet.

I hit her again and once she was down I dragged her into the apartment and tied her up with spare computer cords.

At first, it was amazing. We talked for hours—well I talked, Cathy occasionally moaned and grunted and chomped at me if I came too close. With her undivided attention, I finally professed the words of love I dared not utter before, holding her cold stiff hand and gazing into her droopy eyes.

I cooked for her, but she didn't seem interested in Mac n' Cheese or Hot Pockets. Cathy was attentive when I played videos games though, her eyes locked on the TV screen. She didn't even criticize when I screwed up.

The best time was when I read her my poetry, starting with the stuff I wrote in high school, so she could really get a sense of my progression as an artist. Eventually I mustered up the courage to read the poems I'd written for her: "Laundry Day Rendezvous" and "Evening of Ecstasy." She was so quiet, obviously entranced by my lyrical metaphors and artful alliteration. She understood what I was feeling in my soul. It was great.

Soon, it felt a little less great. I strained to hold one-sided conversations. Cathy's constant moaning kept me up at night, and not in the way I wanted. Her hunger for my body wasn't exactly what I had in mind either and as kinky as it was to have her tied up, I just didn't think it would work for the long term. Though I hate to say it, she wasn't looking her best: her ratty hair was falling out in clumps, her eyes were now gray and blood shot, and she was drooling constantly.

As an escape, I watched more TV. This morning I watched a special about the outbreak. According to new research, it was only spread through body fluids, usually via a non-fatal bite.

Just to be clear: I thought about this a lot. I weighed the pros and cons and even made a list, but this was my chance. I wanted Cathy for so long and then something like this happens—a miracle to bring us together. Destiny.

I sat down across from Cathy and took her hand.

"Cathy, I want to be with you forever, but I'm gonna need a little bite first. Can you do that for me?"

She grunted, her head rolling to the side. I raised my arm. Her eyes lit up as she clamped onto my flesh. The pain was extraordinary, and I had to beat her with the didgeridoo until she let go.

I eased down onto the couch, staring at the chunk missing from my arm. Cathy screamed, my blood oozing from her mouth as she thrashed her arms trying to break free.

My hand is a little shaky and I'm trying my best not to smear blood on this, but my head feels a bit cloudy and I figured I should

FILE 8962: FOUND IN APARTMENT 211

get this down now, just so you know why. I'm not crazy. I'm just in love. Besides, with this much desire between us, the sex will be amazing.

Tiffany E. Wilson developed a fascination for the weird and bizarre as a young girl. Since then she's drawn from that interest to write strange and humorous stories. She lives in Chicago with her boyfriend, a rabbit, and a chinchilla.

Warmth Within thy Depths
Kenneth W. Cain

HE LIVED FOR MOMENTS LIKE THIS; when the ocean embraced him, with only the faint echo of his own breath for comfort. This peaceful bliss was the reason he started diving in the first place. The inner sanctity that was the result of it was both reflective and growing. He took a deep breath and let it out slowly, allowing his lungs to compress properly before descending further into the darkness.

At twenty meters John paused, flicked the light of his mask on, and continued to descend. He felt as if he were falling through the sky as he drifted down. With less of the sun reaching the water there, it began to get colder as if warning him to stay away, but of course John would not listen. This was where he felt most comfortable.

It's okay baby, he thought as if talking to the water, *I will not be long*, but he knew that was a lie. Truth was, he was not sure how long he would be. When he got down this far, he often lost himself to the wonders of the surreal world he loved so much.

Near fifty meters down was where John got his first look at the floor as it sloped down at a sharp angle. He could see something new this time however, and moved in to inspect. What he had thought a fissure at first, was actually a large impact area. From the impact point, a trail of debris ran off down the slope, made up of broken sea structures that had been in the way. What they had been in the way of he was not sure, but he hoped to find out, and to some degree this additional adventure excited John.

He let himself bounce along down the slope, watching that the debris did not impair his own path. Along the way, he inspected

WARM WITHIN THY DEPTHS

the large formations of reef rock that the debris came from. Each brought him more confidence that he would soon find the cause of this disturbance, but as he reached the end of the trail, he found nothing.

Where the slope righted itself upon the ocean floor, there was a large indentation, but nothing of significance beyond that. John inspected the area, looking for clues of what could have happened. He wondered if whatever it had been might have taken on some sort of buoyancy and been set adrift, but then thinking about the destruction surrounding the impact area, he pushed the thought away. Even if it had, he was sure that he would at least find more broken debris in the surrounding area crowded with sea life. Yet, there was none.

A small school of blue fish flew past him to his left, and he turned his head to catch them, but what he saw beyond them is what held his attention. Along the left side of slope was a small opening.

At the foot of the cave was some disrupted rock and John bent down to inspect it closer. He saw nothing different about the rock itself, but what he did find odd, was a metal shaving. He inspected it for a moment and then dropped it, deciding to follow the debris trail.

That task was easy to start, as the opening to the cave was large enough for him to fit in. Further in it became more difficult as the walls of the cave tightened in on him, barely wide enough for John to squeeze through. The tunnel turned upwards, and he heaved himself up, using his feet at times to help until he came to a larger opening of water where he found something extraordinary.

Although there was complete darkness, he was well aware that his head was not feeling that constant pressure of water around it. Knowing this, he thought he might have come up in some sort of air pocket and adjusted the light on his mask in trying to see more clearly.

The room around him glowed in the direction he was looking. Light found a wall that seeped a thin layer of slimy water across a platform of rocks and then into the pool where he now floated.

Beneath him, where he usually felt safe, an odd sensation came to him. It was one of being watched, as if someone or something had followed him up through the tunnel. It made him uncomfortable, and so he pulled himself up on the platform. Once out of the water, he looked down into the pool and after finding nothing, took a moment to look around.

Being as his mask had begun to fog up, it was becoming difficult to see. This made him a bit anxious, so he removed the mask and took in a deep breath of the stale air the cavern offered. The quality of air was not as bad as he had thought it would be, but it definitely did not flow enough to keep it fresh. The slow trickle of water down the walls helped to oxygenate it some though, so it was tolerable. Even then that uneasy feeling seemed overwhelming as he sat on the ledge clearing his thoughts.

Holding it in his hand, he turned the mask's light against each wall, careful to inspect them closely. The cavern seemed about fifteen feet wide and near thirty in length. Not being able to see the ceiling clear enough, he stood up trying to get a better vantage point. But no matter what he did, he could not get enough light on it.

John reached into his suit and pulled out a pack of cigarettes and a lighter. A long hard drag off of a cigarette would suit him fine to steady his nerves. The cigarette lit easy, and he took a deep drag, letting his lungs hold it before exhaling a large puff of smoke. The cloud hovered motionless for a second, before circulating in the air and dispersing as if something had disturbed it. He looked down at the water surface, turning his mask light on it as well and watched as a small swirl dissipated into a flat motionless bed of water.

John reached back into his suit and began to tear off a small section of his shirt, struggling to not damage his suit in the process. The sound of the shirt ripping was loud, and it echoed in the cavern, but it was not the only sound he heard. There was something else there as well. *Probably just bats*, he thought to himself, scanning the ceiling as if he could see it. He was sure that he might find one of the winged devils flapping nearby.

He slid his knife from its holster and tied the small piece of shirt around its blade. His attention drew away from it though, hearing a small splash again. He looked back down at the bed of water, turning his light towards it yet again. This swirl of water eased itself into the calmness of the water, same as the last one had. This, he thought, might be the result of bat shit dropping into the water. John did not know as much as most, but he was sure bats never paid much attention to where their crap fell. Thinking this was the cause of the disturbances in the water put his mind at ease a little.

Holding the lighter to the shirt, it caught fire and spread fast up the blade. It was obvious that it would not last long, but he twisted and turned it, holding it towards the ceiling and the far wall where he had not been able to see. There was something up there. He gauged that it might be thirty or so feet high, but also that it was accessible from a group of smaller boulders that had been precariously piled up against it. The strange object appeared to be made from some sort of metal, no doubt the same one that left the shaving in the debris below. Being unsure of what it was, John had little time to consider it as the section of cloth burned out.

John picked up his mask and used what little glow it gave to light the way. He reached the rock formation with little trouble and began climbing towards the metal object. As he climbed, it became clearer, and yet the more he saw, the more questions formed in his head. And then it came into complete focus.

"Oh good lord," the words escaped his mouth in a gasping manner as he tried to maintain his composure. It was either that or risk falling, as his legs began to feel jelly-like, standing at an odd angle to get a better look. He rubbed his eyes and bit his cheek to make sure he was not dreaming, but still the saucer remained.

Making his way up to it, John was even more careful than before, not wanting to disturb it for more reasons than one. When he got close enough, he set his mask down and let his hand caress the metal, tracing its contour as he slid his hand up as far as he could reach. The craft stretched out into the darkness, disappearing into a section of the cavern he could not yet see.

He wondered how it got here and more so he wondered how it had made its way through such a little tunnel. He thought about it for a second, trying different obvious possibilities in his mind, but none of them made any sense but one. It could have been that someone or something had put it here and then built the cavern around it. Perhaps they had put the saucer here in an attempt to hide it.

A low bellow echoed in the room and John spun around, nearly falling in the process. With the feeling growing that he was not alone, he squatted where he was and reached over to dim the light on his mask. He heard something else, a loud pounding noise in his ears. He pressed his fists into them trying to dull the noise, only it did not subside; it got worse. His face flushed, and he felt a sweaty fever rush across it before realizing it was only the excessive beating of his own terrified heart.

Each beat came louder than the last, as it seemed like a countdown to death. *Thump thump,* and of course some hideous creature would ease its twisted gnarly face up from the water. *Thump thump,* and it would eerily crawl up on that same shelf of rock that he had come up on. *Thump thump,* it would sense his presence and of course see him squatting there. *Thump thump,* it would walk towards him drool dripping from its thirsting mouth. Fear would waft up into the air for the creature to wrap its senses around. *Thump,* but there would be no second beat.

The grumbling noise came again - the sound of metal being manipulated or tweaked. The ship behind John hummed in a light,

WARM WITHIN THY DEPTHS

monotonous tone, and a large metallic cracking noise rang in the cavern as the saucer began to move. John felt the rocks that he was squatting on begin to shift ever so slightly, vibrating as something behind him slid open. Now that low grumble came again, only this time it was out in the open, free from its ship. Beyond that low tone was something else too. It was a different noise, like a chorus of higher pitched echoes.

John struggled not to move, but it was difficult as his senses intensified, unable to control themselves. His heart rapped wildly against his ribcage, screaming for relief. The blood rushed through his veins, surging into every limb of his body, making them hot and weak. His face was on fire, dripping of sweat, and anxiousness. His eardrums swelled with pain not only from the beating of his heart, but also from the increasing sensitivity to each sound around him.

Something dropped from the craft to the rocks just above and rolled towards John. Hot, musty air began to drift the odor of it down upon him; the easy breathing of a confident dweller in its home. The rotten smell of decaying flesh and vomit was in each breath, a smell his nose struggled to refuse. The feeling of gagging overwhelmed him, but he held it back in silence. While he knew the creature had not yet sensed him, he was sure the slightest mistake would ensure differently. John shrank into a ball, trying to make himself as small as possible. Hoping not to be seen, he continued to pull in, but as his weight shifted, his foot slid out. His mask went crashing to the rock formation below, where it landed, and the dim light came on.

John knew that he should have looked up to see who or what his company was, but his instinct was to let his eyes follow the falling mask. Where the lit mask had come to lie, he could see two things.

The first was unmistakable and he found it surprising that he had missed it before. It was a single oxygen tank half buried in the rocky structure down close to the landing he had first emerged upon. The other was easier to miss from a low angle, as it would have appeared as a rock. From this vantage point though, he could clearly see that it was a human skull. He let his eyes trace the rock pile towards where he now squatted and counted at least a dozen of such skulls scattered throughout the formation.

The stale smell that filled the room now fueled his fear as the realization began to click. Whatever stood above him had not built this lair to hide anything at all. Instead, it was building its home close to its feeding ground.

He let his eyes dart upward, and they fixated where he thought the creature was, but they found nothing. He brought himself to a standing position ever so careful not to make any noise. His left knee complained with a little pop. Now at full stance, he looked around above him and still found nothing. He knew though—could feel it even—that somewhere in this room there was something with him.

The room spun uneasy as he let himself turn back towards the water and thought about making a break for it, but before he could make the decision to move the noise came yet again. Turning to look, he spun around fast, saw nothing except a glimpse over his shoulder and turned back around to catch it. His cheek smacked against a large mass, and he stumbled back, falling on his ass.

The soft light from his mask below only served to highlight the outline of the creature as it stood before him. It had no arms, save for what appeared as at least a dozen or so appendages squirming from the lower half. Other than that, its torso seemed not unlike that of a man. Although its features could not be fully made out in such little light, a small, bulbous head sat atop the torso. The creature's size alone was most intimidating and John found himself instinctively sinking back against the rocks, among the bones of those that had fallen before him.

It was that quick. Decisions like that always come fast, sometimes too quick, as was the case this time. John dove into the air, towards what he thought would be the pool of water. Only it was not. He hit the rock landing with a ping from his air tank, and perhaps the creature thought he was dead or maybe the odd noise threw it off. Perhaps, it was merely amused by John's futile attempt. Whatever the case, the creature froze for a moment and watched. John looked up writhing in pain as the taste of the warm blood ran down from his forehead to his pressed lips.

He thought to reach for the mask, but it seemed so far away. Being concerned that any obvious movement might change whether the creature would approach, John froze as well. Instead, he waved his hand out behind him until it landed on a solid surface. A cool sensation found his fingertips as he let them blindly trace its contour.

He gripped the tank hard and pulled, easing it into his arms. A quick twist of the nozzle allowed him to ensure enough oxygen remained inside and he shut it. Of course, he could have told that from the weight alone, but he had to be sure.

John pulled a cigarette from his chest pocket as well as the lighter again, only this time he was not looking to smoke it. Tearing the cigarette in half, he took the unfiltered part and stuck it into nozzle of the tank. Using the lighter, he lit the cigarette, and blew on it to encourage a steady ember. Then he eased the tank on just enough to feed the burning cigarette.

As if suspicious, the creature roared in disapproval. John set the tank upright on the platform, crawled to the edge, and rolled into the water. To this action came another roar. He hurried down the tunnel, placing his air hose in his mouth as he did.

Halfway back he began to feel tentacles lashing out at his legs, and he fought to keep them out of the creatures grasp. One seized John's leg and began reeling him backward up the tunnel. He turned and began punching into the darkness, feeling his hands land blows here and there, but unaware of their effectiveness. Most hit solid matter, but one hit something soft, and yet another roar filled the water around him as the creatures grip loosened just long enough for John to make a move.

John swam hard and fast towards where he believed the cave entrance might be, but it was difficult in the darkness. A feeling of freedom overwhelmed him, as the light glow the depths of the open ocean provided, came into view. It was a feeling that did not last long though, as the creature was able to latch onto him again just as he reached the opening to the vast ocean. This time it got both legs and began to drag him back against his will. John turned to look and found himself face to face with his assailant.

At the center of its tentacles, several rows of teeth grinded together in endless procession. They seemed to sharpen themselves in preparation to taste John's flesh as a chef might sharpen his knives before cutting. The mouth was large and torn, tell-tale signs of the struggles it had come across in finding food.

Its body pulsated in the water, a mass of muscle and ribs encasing a stomach that held little regard for its prey. Three large eyes bulged together, a dark liquid stained its tear ducts as if it was crying, but John knew better. Those were not tears of pain. Nor were they from fear. Those, if nothing else, were tears of joy, happiness, and of course hunger. Oh, how he saw hunger in those eyes.

The cave walls felt constricting as he returned to the struggle of getting out. Some of the air escaped his lips, sending a few scattered bubbles up to the surface where he longed to find himself. He used the walls of the cave to brace himself, trying to pull away, but the creature kept pulling and was gaining ground. At this point, John was sure he would lose. That was when the explosion came.

A large boom filled the cave as it began to collapse around the creature. It did not seem as if it were trying to escape though. Instead, the creature flexed its muscles, trying to expand itself as if it were bracing against the collapsing rocks. John watched, confused, as the creature seemed to want to keep the tunnel open as long as it could, willing to sacrifice its life to do so. Only, it was a puzzle that would not go long being unsolved.

WARM WITHIN THY DEPTHS

Three of them came out at once, and John felt surprised at how quick they moved through the water towards him. They were very small and while they initially surprised him, he regained his composure and readied to fight them off with his knife. Behind those, another approached making it four in total. Then two more squeezed out as their mother watched with dark trails of blood running down its face. It was dying to hold the entrance open as long as it could, all the while seeming hungry.

John watched the mother and felt an odd remorse for the creature as it struggled to free its young. He watched as its stomach began to stretch out before it, struggling to release something. That was not it though. It was not trying to release anything. There was something behind it trying to get through.

The creature's stomach burst as the cave began to collapse down upon the dead flesh of the beast. Before the collapse finished, several more young creatures escaped into the open ocean that encompassed John. Now surrounded by more than a dozen of the creatures, John felt as if the ocean had rejected him in spite of his love for it. John looked into their tear-stained eyes and saw no sadness, only hunger. In unison, they turned their tentacles towards him, grinding their teeth in preparation to satisfy their appetite with a taste of his bloodied flesh.

Kenneth W. Cain resides in Eastern Pennsylvania with his wife and two children where he writes dark fiction and horror. Using ingredients he learned while listening to his Grandfather spin tales next to a barrel fire, he now cooks up his own concoctions. A dash of the mysterious, a tablespoon of the unknown and some of those bizarre items from the deepest region of the mental refrigerator are but a few of the elements he uses. You can find out more about this author at his website: www.kennethwcain.com

No Lights
by Alex Azar

NO LIGHTS! NO LIGHTS, NO CLOCK, NO TV, middle of a heat wave, and no AC. I'm really supposed to sleep in a heat wave, with only that damn fan that's perpetually clicking. Click, click, fucking click is all I hear. The entire house is fine, except my room. Apparently, I'm not allowed to watch TV with my AC on in the middle of a heat wave.

Rolling over and over, Greg finds it impossible to find a comfortable position to sleep in atop the cumulating pool of sweat. Stripping down to his boxers, Greg removes his sweat-saturated clothes only to be revolted by the feel of his moist back against the even moister mattress. *That is disgusting. Where's my shirt now?* Replacing the shirt he just took off, unable to find anything else until day breaks through his window. *Still no lights, not even the moon! It's probably only around one and I'm supposed to sleep with no lights and that fan.* 'Hey Greg, if you want to run the fan from my room that's cool, but I don't want to hook up too much to my outlet, no sense in both of us sleeping in the dark, ha!' Yea Haha, real fucking funny Joe. I pay rent like everyone else here but I get screwed.

Still tossing and turning, Greg feels the perspiration seeping through his boxers and imagines himself being found the following morning, drowned in an ocean of his own sweat. *That'd be just lovely, surprise Joe!* The clicking of the fan seems to change tones from time to time; even the pace of the clicking seems to change every so often. *That's all I need, for the fan to die on me.*

NO LIGHTS

Not long after, the clicking of the fan begins to echo across the long cluttered room. The narrowness of the room allowed for one path, a path littered with shoes and sneakers, garbage can and computer chair, even the hovering fan cord. *Shit, even if I could find a way through this mess and out the door, there'd be no other place for me to sleep. Joe, Tony, and Drew's rooms are the only ones with AC and there's no room in them for me to sleep. Maybe if I slept in the living room the TV could drown out the fan.* Just as the thought comes to his mind he hears laughter from down the hall. One voice was clearly Tony's, and the other, Greg figures to be Tony's girl for the night. *Asshole, not only does he have AC in his room he has a new girl in his room every night.* The thought of sleeping on the living room couch vanishes from his mind after realizing the indescribably disgusting things Tony has done on that couch. With the vision of girls, come thoughts of sex, and the sneaking arousal awakens the only part of him that seemed to be asleep. *Well I usually am tired after sex.* And with that Greg slides his hand down his shirt making its way to the elastic of his underwear, but before he reaches his boxers, something tickles his hand. *A bug? What the hell is a bug doing in my room?* Without hesitation, Greg squishes the small, tiny insect between his fingers and drops it next to his bed where he hopes his garbage can is. *That's just nasty; I almost don't want to do this anymore.* But Greg knows he'll never get tired otherwise, so his hand begins the decent again. *Another bug! On my arm... this is nasty.* As he goes to kill this bug he feels another tickle, now on his leg. *You have to be kidding me!* And again before he can kill the 3rd bug, or is it the 4th he wonders, he feels another on his forehead, and his back, shoulder, now his hand. *This is freaking me out.*

Attempting to investigate in the dark, Greg reaches to the side of his bed, against the wall and instantly feels hundreds maybe thousands of bugs crawling up his hand, then arm. *Holy Shit!* Jumping off his bed, Greg lands not on the floor, but on a sea of insects. Ignoring the cuts he knows are on his feet, Greg steadily walks to the door, knocking over the garbage can. The crunching and chattering of the bugs deafen the sound of the clicking fan, but that is no comfort to Greg. Tripping over a sneaker, or shoe, Greg falls and tangles his leg in the chair. *Ow damn it; I think I broke my ankle. Those bastards are crawling all over me. Damn it, in my ears, nose, and mouth. Crap, I can't get up. Think, think ow shit they're eating me. What the hell are these things? What am I gonna do?* Quickly thinking, Greg maps out the lightless room, and positions himself next to the computer desk. *Damn it, there's nothing there, ow!*

Still being attacked, Greg realizes if his computer desk is on his right; to his left must be his dresser. *My dresser, my dresser... yes my dresser! My lighter, gotta reach my lighter.* Fighting the pain in his ankle and infinite bug wounds. Greg pulls himself up and swipes his hand across the littered dresser until he finds his lighter. *Alright let's see these things.* Igniting the lighter, Greg can't see any bugs - it's as if they can perfectly avoid the light. He still feels the bites, assuring him they're still there. Still in pain, still thinking. *Cologne! Yes that'll do it!* Searching the dresser a second time Greg finds the cologne faster than he did the lighter. *Let's see you avoid this you pieces of shit!* Spraying the cologne through the lighter's flame, Greg still can't hear the clicking fan, still feels pain, but there is still no light. Nonetheless, Greg knows it's working and with a triumphant laugh *HA HA HA!!!!* Greg whips his makeshift flamethrower across the room, killing bug after bug, dozens at a time. But the pain doesn't relent, in fact it doubles, even triples; intensifying, multiplying along with the crackling sound and burning smell. A vile smell forces Greg's stomach to turn, but the pain is too much to allow him to vomit. *Have to get out of here,* are his only thoughts, as the pain takes over. Escaping was his only thought, not contemplation of why no one had come to his aid, only escape - an escape that is never realized.

NO LIGHTS

Alex Azar is an author born and raised in New Jersey. After attending a technical school for two years and taking every English course offered there, he knew writing was not only his passion but his future.

Insomnia
A.A. Garrison

"You break it, you bought it."
-- *Store-hung signs innumerable*

Friday

"LOUDER!" SOMEONE CRIED, and the blaring music somehow grew more so. Every bass note punched Pete's chest, and he liked it.

Stan was in the middle of the room, taking beer from an apparatus. "Oh!" he hooted after struggling it down. Pete's dog, Sally, answered with a bark.

Pete took his own tour of duty with the beer apparatus -- he refused to call it a bong -- and then circuited the rental house's cavernous living room, talking, laughing, dancing discursively with the soused girls Stan had produced. Something happened on the TV, and Stan said, "Oh!" Sally barked.

Pete's world spun and blurred, and suddenly he had the red-white-and-blue package of fireworks leftover from the Fourth, and he was outside, and it was cold but he was too numb to feel it, and he was asking one of the manshapes with him for a light.

Staggering down the sloped gravel driveway, Pete claimed one of the many discarded beer bottles and fitted a Roman candle inside. For no fathomable reason, he then lit it, aimed the bottle at the night sky, and let the missile fly. With a flash, the projectile wished from the bottle and across the street, like a firefly gone nuclear, Pete thought. It whined a one-note crescendo in the key of waking-infant, loud enough to conquer the screaming music, and then exploded in an uninspired spray of sun-colored light directly above the ugly house across the street.

The drunken college students cheered, Stan went "Oh!" and Sally barked. The clock read 2:39 AM.

Saturday

Pete awoke with evil in his head, incisive late-morning sun on his face. He moaned and attempted a retreat into sleep, but he was awake. Voices murmured from downstairs. It was almost eleven, but it felt like five.

"Hey, Sleeping Beauty," Stan said as Pete stumbled down the shag stairway. Stan seemed awful chipper for such a morning after, but he always did; he could not only drink Pete under the table, but dodge any hint of consequence. He was dressed for work, in his wonted pharmacy smock.

"Shove it," Pete croaked, and flipped a halfhearted bird. He tripped on the last step but recovered ungracefully, animating his chubby frame.

Stan flung more zingers as Pete, oblivious, scared up breakfast, vines of hangover snatching at him. Oddments of the night's party conversed in the breakfast nook, a sleep-tousled girl and a couple guys Pete didn't know, and Pete ignored them, breakfasting sourly. Sally cantered over, broom-grass tail wagging, and he lightened some, showing the dog some attention in between bites. There was always time for Sally, come hell or high water. The grinning collie had materialized at the rental property during freshman year, dirty and skinny and palpably lost, and though Pete was known to abhor all things breathing -- himself included -- he had taken to the dog. The two made a good pair, according to Stan, since both enjoyed eating and shitting and sniffing ass, and neither would ever see a woman naked. Stan also thought, privately, that Pete and Sally shared the commonality of a sheltered existence; Pete's half of the rent came by way of his father's checks, as did everything else.

"You tell him yet?" one of the party-guys said to Stan. His eyes lit furtively on Pete, then cut away.

Pete straightened from Sally. "Tell me what?"

No one said anything, and no one would meet Pete's eyes. They acted as if asked to help clean up a mess.

"Tell me what?" Pete asked again, appealing the little crowd.

"Your car," Stan said, finally. He gave Pete a sober look. "Someone, eh, someone dicked with it."

Pete's hangover leapt up. "What about my car?"

Stan set down his plate of eggs and toweled his mouth. "Come on," he said, and solemnly started for the door.

Pete followed, Sally at his heel. The party people said nothing.

* * * * *

The day was majestically clear, a study in Appalachian autumn. The two-bedroom rental house was sited on a small promontory, nestled in a shady crib of oaks and pines. The leaves had peaked already, but the bronzed remnants remained beautiful in their own right. Pete saw none of it, however: he was fixated on his cherished Jaguar sedan, parked down by the road. The car, Dad's high-school graduation present, was the showpiece of his twenty-one-year-old ego, and any injury it sustained was shared by him in physicality, much as twins receive each other's afflictions.

Shading his eyes with his hand, Pete gave the car a quick once-over from the stoop. It appeared intact, sleeping at the foot of the driveway, but he was too far away to be sure. The sharp incline scorned the Jaguar's two-wheel drive, as well as some four-wheel-drives, so the landlord had furnished the lot with an auxiliary parking area along the road. Pete burst from the porch and down the steep little hill buffering the house from the blacktop, Sally in pursuit.

INSOMNIA

"What's wrong with it?" Pete asked as he bounced down the cut, chafing with each step.

"You've been keyed," Stan said grimly, and stopped at the gloss-black trunk. He nodded to the driver's side, eyes narrowed.

Pete dashed to the car and froze, arms vaguely akimbo. An obtuse scratch spanned the length of the left side, painfully visible in the harsh sun. It looked like a child's attempt at a racing stripe.

Pete was initially speechless, and then he cursed, loud enough to echo off the split-logged house looming across the street.

* * * * *

Nighttime, and Pete lay in bed, brooding. It was late, around twelve, and he was tired, but each attempt at sleep was thwarted by the thought of some asshole's key raping his Jag. Still, in time he wandered into unconsciousness, slowly unmooring from bitter reality ... then the phone rang.

Pete's eyes sprung open. After a soupy second, he slithered his hand to the crying handset, lifted it to his ear, and muttered a hello.

No answer.

Pete said hello again, and after hearing only the insect-like buzz of the line, he let the phone fall to its cradle and flounced back into bed.

Sunday

Pete hunched in the breakfast nook, a plate of eggs and toast cooling on the table. A baptismal rain assaulted the house, coming in thunderous sheets. He picked absently at the food while toiling through the yellow half of his and Stan's phonebook. They'd spilt beer on it at some point, and it was hard to part the Bible-thin pages. Sally sat faithfully to his left, tail beating the floor.

After deliberating the area's five available body shops, Pete settled on one and scribbled down a number. He'd call it tomorrow.

Footsteps thudded down the stairs, and Stan appeared in the kitchen. Sunday was his day off, and he always slept late.

"Hey, Sleeping Beauty," Pete said, with a toothy smile. Sleep had done him good, enough for his wise-ass nature to reassert itself.

"Mornin'," Stan said, and bee-lined for the coffee machine.

Sally trotted over to pay her respects, but Stan ignored her -- he had stopped rigidly at the bay window overlooking the driveway. "Pete," he said, gravely.

Pete looked from the phonebook, his face recording Stan's tone. "What?" he asked, and at once thought of the Jag, that hateful scratch.

"Your car," Stan said, and gave Pete a grave look. The rain sheeted over the window.

Pete was up and at the door in seconds flat. He tore it open, swiped a seldom-used umbrella, and ran pell-mell outside, his slippers cracking the puddled deck. Fighting open the umbrella, he barreled rotundly down the driveway and then stopped halfway, seized with horror: the Jaguar looked to have suffered a wreck. The windshield frowned in a concave slump, white with a spider web of fractures. The car rested at a lazy angle that implied flat tires. The light played off the body all wrong, bespeaking dents. All five windows were honked out, a snow of glass shards surrounding the orifices. Stan's Volvo station wagon sat at its wing, untouched.

Pete slogged toward the car, his steps queered with shock. He made plosive noises during his approach, what sounded like, "My cuh, my cuh." Grimacing, he rounded the trunk and found that the tires were indeed slashed, the polished rims touching earth. Rain guttered through the window-shaped wounds, pooling in the leather seats. In the driver's seat, however, there was something more: a long brown rope of turd, patently human.

INSOMNIA

Pete shifted on his feet, swaying like a charmed snake. His knuckles went white over the umbrella's rattan handle. The plosive noises stopped, and his face became a ticking bomb.

Before he could explode, however, a motor sounded from behind, followed by an opening car door. Rousted from his anger, Pete turned to find his neighbor's rusted Dodge pickup truck, across the road in its gravel-pit parking spot. The door opened wider and a tall, spectacularly thin figure stepped out, dressed in green-stained BibAlls that jibed with the confusion of lawn-mowing equipment in the truck's bed.

Pete left his annihilated car and stomped across the street, blind to any potential traffic. "Hey!" he shouted to his neighbor, who he'd never officially met in the three years he and Stan had been living next door. "Hey!"

The ragged man stood reticently beside his rust-mottled truck, resigned to the rain. Uninflected blue eyes stared from a seamed face, framed in inky sockets. Vitreous black licks of hair stuck to his head.

Pete stopped an awkward two feet from the soaking man. "Somebody ..." he said, but the rest wouldn't come. Something about his mute neighbor made the words impact in his throat. He pointed instead. "My car," he managed. "Somebody ... *hurt*, my *car*." He was stammering. "Did you see?" His neighbor's towering house overlooked the crime scene.

The man's pained eyes went to the violated sports car, then back to Pete. "Someone took a sledge to it, looks like," he said, his lips barely parting. He might have thrown his voice.

When the man said nothing more, Pete replied: "Yeah, looks like it. You see anything last night? Or the night before? Because ..." He trailed off, drunk with grief and anger. Spray from the rain misted his body.

The neighbor stared, a sheen layer of rain on his face. "Can't say I did," he said after a pause, again with that ventriloquist repose.

Poignantly disappointed in the way only the overweight can manage, Pete nodded and gave an agnostic thank-you, then scrambled inside to call the police. The other man walked slowly to his big brown house, the rain pelting him.

* * * * *

It was two in the morning, and Pete held no illusions regarding sleep. The vandalism had struck a foul chord in him, boiling his guts. The responding police officer had, with clinical detachment, said they'd probably never catch the culprit, and Pete believed him. The cop had disposed of the shit, at least, taking it in some tongs and flinging it to the woods like a dead snake.

Pete camped at his bedroom window, scowling in Friday's clothes. He continually got up to check the car, hoping he'd catch the cocksucker going for a trifecta. The storm had passed and the moon was out, affording the world a ghostly, cheese-colored tint. The defiled car sat center stage, its windows fitted with plastic, waiting for the wrecker to come haul it off. Dad would take care of the repairs, sure, just like Dad took care of the rent and the credit cards and the tuition. But it was no consolation: Pete had an enemy now, and a cowardly one at that (with a healthy digestive tract, too, given the kilter of the stool).

He cycled through different potentials, anyone who may have found an axe to grind with young Peter Santos. He was a jackass, admittedly -- at his weight, it was either Class Clown or Class Reject, and he'd chosen the former -- and he was sure there was no shortage of possible adversaries around campus; but he couldn't see anyone taking it this far, especially considering the ugly postscript. Whacking the hell out of a car is one thing, but it takes some real malice to make Number Two in someone's driver's seat.

Sighing, he admired the bohemian house across the street. The place was strangely made, and no less weird in the moonlight. Pregnant gutters sagged beneath a rug of mossy shingles, lending it the dilapidated air of an old man's skin. Its cold black windows seemed to stare back, depthless as horse eyes. A cupola sprigged

INSOMNIA

from the roof like a little head, punctuated by round stained-glass windows that looked out of place. The haggard man he'd talked to that afternoon was the only person Pete had ever seen around the place. The guy barely went out, and was always in his verdant lawnmower-man fatigues when he did. He kept his distance from Pete and Stan, and they him, but Pete had seen him up close several times, always at the parking lot. The guy was perpetually wan, radiating sickness like Holocaust victims Pete had seen. Pete judged him in his thirties or thereabouts, but he looked older, thanks to his consumptive temperament. The guy went with his house, Pete thought, each being tall and awkward and alone. It was sad, really. Good thing Pete couldn't care less.

He stole one last glance out the window and drew the curtains, reluctantly making for bed. Riled as Pete was, the Sandman was making himself known. He collapsed heavily over the mattress, and commenced the job of forgetting the Jag and baiting his mind to rest. And though he never really accomplished this -- the gelded car kept leapfrogging from the back of his head -- he was tired from all the excitement, and sleep took him anyway.

Then the phone rang.

Pete levered upright, one cheerless eye peeling open. He dubiously regarded the phone, and it rang again.

Movement stirred from the bedroom across the hall. Stan. "Get the phone!" he roared, slurred with unrest. He didn't have a phone in his bedroom; the jack had died and had yet to be fixed.

There was another importune ring, and Pete manhandled the handset to his ear and said hello. When there was no immediate answer, he hung up, hard. It made him remember the call he'd received last night; his skin prickled, and he stared at the phone for nearly a minute.

Pete gradually laid down, going supine without looking away from the phone, and no sooner had his head touched the pillow than the phone rang again. If he didn't know better, he'd say the caller could see him.

Unamused, he at once snatched it up and barked another hello, loud enough to be doubled in the caller's handset. When there was again no answer, Pete reacted with the natural questions, asking who the caller was, what they wanted, the words coming in a gibbering rush. He then relinquished a bald "Stop calling here!" and slammed the phone home. He checked the caller ID as an afterthought, but there was only a cul-de-sac PRIVATE. He flounced angrily onto his stomach, imprecating into his pillow.

Then, not a minute later, the phone rang again.

Livid, Pete grabbed the handset and, without putting it to his ear, screamed to be left alone. He then hammered it to the hook, landing it crooked and not caring. It soon began burping a hang-me-up noise, and Pete righted it.

"Who is it?" Stan moaned from the next room, and Pete told him to shut up and go to sleep.

This time Pete didn't lie down; he slouched against the headboard, cooking in his own juices. He wanted to punch something; badly. A voice from the well of his head suggested that this was somehow connected to the car, but he quashed it; to accept such would be too much to bear. Internally, he insisted the phone shenanigans were only some random shit-head having fun, just like whoever had rampaged his car. Sally came in then, and Pete pet her briskly, working her ears like a string of worry beads. In time, her presence defrayed the anger enough for him to kill the light and again attempt sleep.

A half-hour passed and an irenic quiet fell, but just as the first swirls of dreamscape tugged at Pete's brain, the phone rang a third time.

Stan groaned, and Pete savaged the phone from its cradle, this time saying nothing. He only listened, his eyes darting busily around the room. The line was alive, as evidenced by ambient noises and a faint cackle that could be breathing, and he waited for a long minute. He grasped for something to say, some vituperation to scare the son of a bitch into leaving him alone; he had time to

INSOMNIA

parse his mental diary of four-letter words and disparaging phrases, but nothing came, at least nothing with the clout he needed.

Then, as he settled on some empty threats rich with F-bombs, a plangent sound burst from the earpiece, what could have been a siren run through a bullhorn. It was loud enough to vibrate the phone in his hand.

Pete bleated with surprise and dropped the handset, the commotion unlimbering Sally from the bed. The gooselike honk continued for a moment after, loud even from the floor -- but that wasn't all. There was more to the noise, Pete heard, another dimension to it, as though he was receiving it in stereo. The honk lasted only a couple more seconds, but it was enough to discern its other component as coming from just outside; from across the street, perhaps.

He reclaimed the phone, now dead, and put it on the hook. His right ear sung a high C. His heart punched blood. His scrotum was tight as a drumhead. He swallowed and tasted blood -- he'd bit his tongue.

He eventually returned to bed, and even though the phone slept, Pete didn't.

Monday

Pete awoke groggy and disjointed, like a record spun backwards and too fast. He had scrounged a few broken winks towards daybreak, but the weekend's aggregate sleep loss was making itself felt. He was hung-over and sluggish, like he'd pulled one of Stan's famous benders. Everything lay beneath a snide wrap of unreality, and the car crisis helped none.

After forcing a perfunctory breakfast, he called the body shop and they sent a guy right out. The wrecker arrived within minutes, and it helped some seeing the car hauled off, like getting a sick family member out of the house. Pete called home after, to deliver the news, and Dad was outraged in his special way. He said he'd "make some calls," whatever that meant, and was quick to okay a rental car for his Petey. Pete, playing Good Son, thanked him and said he loved him, and the two hung up.

Stan gave him a lift to the car-rental place on the way to the pharmacy, and Pete's new ride, a cherry-red Subaru that couldn't hold a candle to the Jag, was waiting for him when he arrived. He went to the university from there, feeling stupid in the faggy car, and the morning's two classes were disasters, four hazy hours spent learning nothing. However, by the time he quit the campus and started home, he was at last coping with his victim status, as the human animal is wont to do. When he pulled the crummy rental into the home's roadside parking lot, he had actually begun forgetting his traumatic weekend.

Then he found the firework.

As he climbed onto the porch, lusting after some lunch, he discovered what looked like a burnt candy cane on his doormat. Puzzled, he went on his haunches and gave the thing a long, searching look, the same he may have shown a flying saucer. He picked it up and it was a Roman candle, spent, of the same kind he foggily remembered firing off during Friday night's party. He tweezed it with two fingers and raised it myopically to his face, unsure what to make of its sudden appearance on his doorstep.

Before he could give it more thought, though, he stepped inside and forgot all about it: Sally wasn't at the door. She was always there when he came home from class, waiting for her squat in the grass. He canvassed the house, moving with the celerity of a much smaller man, and came up empty.

Sally was missing.

* * * * *

More rain had blown in, and it bleared Pete's view of the house across the street, rendering it a runny brown phantom. Night was falling.

INSOMNIA

"That fuck did it," he said to Stan, not looking from the window. "He busted up my car, and now he's got Sally." He spoke in a hushed, exacting tone, contrary to the brutality of his words.

"You need to get off that," Stan said for the third time, entertaining a steaming plate of ribs. It was suppertime, and he was the only one eating. "You've got no proof. Sally could've just run off."

"Because you had the door open for two minutes," Pete said, sounding unconvinced.

"Because I had the door open for two minutes," Stan agreed. He'd been home earlier in the day, to change clothes after work, and had admitted to leaving the door open while he did so. "That's all the time it would've taken. You know how she is, always jonesing to get outside." He bit into a fresh rib, holding it in both hands like a weird ear of corn.

"And the firework?" Pete retorted.

Stan raised his hands, the rib waving like a wand. "I dunno. Maybe the guy left it there to make a statement. I mean, you did shoot the damn thing at his house."

Pete quit the window. "It was a statement, all right," he growled. "'I have your dog.' That's the statement."

"Okay, Sherlock," Stan mocked, chewing. "If you're so sure, then go ask him." He gestured across the street, using his whole head, "go ask him."

There was a thinking pause, and Pete shrunk a little. "Okay, maybe I will."

Stan gestured again, now with the rib. "Guy's truck is there now." He looked pleased with himself. "Have at it."

Pete mumbled, "Smartass," and grabbed his shoes.

Stan dropped his shoulders. "Come on, man," he said, discarding the rib to the graveyard on his plate. "The guy doesn't have your dog, and he didn't smash up the Jag. Chill out."

But Pete was already outside.

* * * * *

The night was damp and miserable, in the way only fall rains can be, and Pete staggered uncertainly down the driveway, his turquoise umbrella in one hand and the blackened Roman candle in the other. The homes' conflicting floodlights lit his way.

He passed his ruddy rental car and Stan's Volvo, then stopped along the curb, the rain drenching his tennis shoes. His neighbor's three-story manor rose before him, now menacing and contemptuous, like an adult as perceived by a child. From Pete's low vantage, its array of windows glowered rather than stared, lidless eyes sinister in character. A car sloshed around the bend, and Pete crossed the road after it had gone by.

His path took him around his neighbor's heap of a truck and into a patchy lawn. The lawn overlooked a cinderblock abutment enabling a short driveway, the tongue of asphalt branching from the main road to a garage. Pete had never noticed it before, the driveway or the garage, and it bolstered the house's size, making him feel very small.

He boarded the home's arcaded stoop and lowered his umbrella, instantly feeling like an intruder. A baseless fear closed over him, and he considered just turning back, letting the cops handle it ... but then he thought of Sally, held hostage by this dick, and went on. The door was an unassuming white fiberglass job, an economy choice, probably, and he knocked twice. There was a moment of nothing, the rain peppering the shingles, and then slow movement came from inside and the door cracked open, an inquiring blue eye caught in the slit.

There was a tense moment when neither man spoke, Pete suffering the scrutiny of that single discarnate eyeball. Then, when he finally found his tongue, Pete realized he didn't know his neighbor's name. He now felt dumb as well as small, unequipped for this encounter.

"Help you?" a scratchy voice said.

"Hello, yes," Pete said evenly, as though he were addressing his grandfather. All the fight had left him. "I'm your neighbor, Pete

INSOMNIA

Santos" -- he jerked a thumb over his shoulder -- "and I was wondering if you may've seen my dog."

The door opened further, and the eye gained a mate. There was a frothy pink hue in the whites, Pete saw, like bloody mucus. Besides an insular mote of cheek, the rest of the man was clothed in shadow. "Pete Santos," he said reflectively, the mouth unseen.

Pete nodded. An expectant silence spun out and he felt like he should say something, but there was nothing else to say. He tried to see inside, but it was too dark.

The eyes made some assessing movements, and then locked back on Pete's. "What's that in your hand there, Pete?"

Pete raised the Roman candle as though just finding it. "Oh, that. I found it, on my step," he stuttered. "I was wondering if maybe, you, I dunno, found it, and ... put it there?" This was going badly.

More silence between the two, the rain too loud. Pete again felt that the ball was in his court, even though it wasn't.

"Someone been firin' off firecrackers," the man said at last, and the eyes narrowed some, pronouncing their oily sockets. "Maybe them fellers down the street. Buncha collegeCollege kids down there, always playin' loud music. Keeps me up at night ..."

There was another rental house around the bend, but Pete had never heard music coming from it, loud or otherwise. He went black with guilt. "Yeah, maybe ... them, from down the street," he said, unable to meet the evil blue eyes.

"Ain't seen no dog," the eyes said, with a note of finality.

Pete gave a nervous nod, making brief eye contact and then looking away. "Okay, well, she's a collie, a purebred, name's Sally. Just in case you, you know ..."

"Sally, collie," the eyes repeated. "My name's Cody. John Cody. I'll keep an eye out."

Pete nodded again, shaking his bangs. "Okay, thank you, Mister Cody, thank you." He felt like saying "Thank you" again, for some reason.

"Well. I best be gettin' to bed. It's late."

Pete agreed that it was late, despite it being barely eight o'clock.

"Night, Pete Santos," John Cody said, and the door shut before Pete could answer.

* * * * *

Pete spent the night combing his sparse neighborhood for Sally, and after three hours, she was still missing and he was too hoarse to call for her any more. Stan was in bed when Pete came home.

Pete didn't need any help staying awake that night, but the phone calls came anyway: eight total, spaced in tactical thirty-minute intervals. With each, Pete wearily raised and lowered the handset, perhaps expecting to find something underneath. He spent the gist of the night at the window, thinking of Sunday night, when he'd heard that bullhorn-noise blowing both from the phone and the house next door.

He did sleep, around five, and his last thought was of shooting off the Roman candle, seeing it sputter and die over John Cody's roof as it wailed like a punched baby.

Tuesday

"Okay, okay, just calm the hell down," Stan said, and stared thoughtfully at the Polaroid picture sitting over the dining table.

Pete turned back to the window. He'd been spending a lot of time there. "I can't calm down, dammit," he said in a low voice that betrayed his anger. "He fucked with my car, and then he took Sally, and now he's been in our house." He took a ruminative sip of coffee, bloodshot eyes trained abrasively across the street.

Stan sighed and looked back to the Polaroid, as if it may provide an answer. He felt around for some rebuttal, for his own sake as much as Pete's, but there were none. The picture depicted Pete's bed, unmade from the night, as he'd left it before going to class that morning. According to Pete, he'd come home that afternoon and found it tucked innocently in the door. An hour later, Stan had come home to find Pete stamping around the house, looking like something from Night of the Living Dead. Stan had tried to calm him, but it was getting harder and harder to dismiss the situation as benign, especially after Pete related his tracing the crank call to the house across the street. It seemed Pete had made a friend.

Stan frowned at the Polaroid, kneading his temples. "First, we call the police," he said, doubled over the table. The rain raged, laying a premature dark over the world.

Pete sipped his coffee, his eyes on the house. "And then?"

"I don't know," Stan snapped, now sounding a little like Pete. "You can start locking the door, for one." It was one of Pete's foibles, neglecting to lock up when he left for class; Stan hounded him on it, despite his habit of leaving the door wide open. "How many times have I told you ...?" Stan started, then trailed off when Pete turned around: Pete looked like shit, as though run over by a bus, maybe. "Just start locking the door, please," Stan finished, in a different voice.

Pete made no reply.

* * * * *

The cop was the same who'd taken the report on Pete's car, a tall, beefy guy who looked to be cottered into his bulletproof vest. He was at first skeptical to Pete's claims, but after hearing his case -- the phone calls, the stereo bullhorn, the bad-penny firework, the unsettling Polaroid, Sally -- he gave an acquiescent nod and started another report. He confiscated both the used firework and the Polaroid, putting them into big yellow bags marked **EVIDENCE**. At Pete's insistence, the cop went across the street for a *tête-à-tête* with Mr. Cody.

Pete, ever the voyeur, watched the drama play out over Cody's stoop, a replay of last night's farcical interrogation. The cop stood in the doorway for less than five minutes, then left, the door shutting behind him. Pete bristled like a spooked cat.

That night, Sally had still not come home, and more phone calls came. Pete did not sleep.

Wednesday

It was morning, raining still, and Stan padded into the kitchen, spiffy in his pharmacy smock. He leaned surreptitiously through the doorway to see if Pete was still at the window. He was, unmoved since last night.

"Hey," Stan called tentatively, and started breakfast.

Pete made a sound in greeting, not turning from the window.

Stan fixed and ate his meal without saying anything more to the revenant at the windowsill. When he had finished and done the dishes, however, he checked the clock and said, "Don't you have a nine o'clock?" It was eight fifteen, and Pete was in sweatpants.

"Yep," Pete said. Only his mouth moved.

"Shouldn't you be getting ready?"

"Yep."

Stan took a contemplating pause, then said, "Pete. Come on. You can't let this guy destroy your life." He made for his friend, but as he got within striking distance, Pete turned and fixed him with a look that could melt candles. Pete was a wreck, even worse than last night. Purple bags under his eyes, hair in an oily mohawk, lips chapped. He had surpassed road kill, Stan thought: Pete now resembled something eaten and shat.

Stan stopped and, after some nonverbal communication, backed away. "Pete, come on, dude ..." he said in a small voice that didn't carry.

"He took Sally," Pete said, and rotated deliberately back to the window. The outside veneer of rain deformed his reflection. "He's not taking anything else."

Stan stood there a moment longer, then went to work.

INSOMNIA

* * * * *

The day passed, the rain fell, and John Cody remained in his indecorous house. Pete was sure of it, because, except for ten seconds to fetch a bucket and some toilet paper, he hadn't left his post at the window. His eyes hurt, and so did his back, but they failed to bother him. He was hungry and thirsty and sleepy, too, but, at the same time ... he wasn't. Every so often his left eyelid twitched. He smelled unpleasant. It was four-thirty in the afternoon.

A cordless phone chirped from the table behind Pete, and he made no move for it. Only after the third clangorous ring did he retrieve it and check the caller ID: MATT'S GARAGE. He answered.

"Hello," he said darkly, abstaining from any shred of conviviality.

"Yo, Mister Santos?" said the harried male voice on the other end, presumably Matt.

Pete said yes.

"Your Jag's ready."

Pete straightened for the first time in two days, slapped out of his twilight. "Ready," he said, incredulous.

"Yep," Matt said. Then, perhaps reading Pete's surprise: "Your pop's a good guy."

Dad had made another call, apparently. Pete asked when he could pick it up.

"Now," Matt said a little too quickly, suggesting he needed the space.

Pete passed a conflicted look between the phone and the dripping house across the street. "Give me thirty minutes," he said. "I've gotta return my rental car first."

Matt said that was fine, and the two hung up.

* * * * *

Following a lead-footed race down to town and back, complete with several narrowly averted collisions, a four-block jog, and a very brief encounter with Matt, Pete returned to the sequestered acre he shared with Mr. John Cody. He drove his refurbished car hesitantly around the final bend, half expecting to find Cody waiting with a sledgehammer and an eager bowel. He stopped just beyond the properties, squinting to see through the misty curtain of dusk. Nothing had changed, except John Cody's spavined truck was missing from the driveway. Pete didn't know if this was good or bad.

He parked and left the car running; the umbrella was in the house. Wearing a fresh coat of rain, he stormed his doormat and began fishing his windbreaker for the key -- then remembered that he'd forgotten to lock the door. Again. Stan would be pissed, but Stan didn't need to know. He grabbed the handle too hard, in a hurry to resume his surveillance, and the door opened on its own. It hadn't been latched.

It was completely dark inside, and he clawed for the light, visions of psychotic neighbors crowding his head. Finding the switch in an explosion of white, he slipped defensively into the home's tiny foyer, devoting equal attention to the adjoining dining room and the world at his back. He closed the door, turning the knob as to be unheard, and prowled inside, hands knifed out at his sides as if struggling for balance. He repressed an urge to yell hello.

Standing in the doorway of the dining room, he angled his head left and right, and everything looked in order. Over the table was a plastic grocery-store bag he didn't recognize, but he ignored it, preferring to sweep the house first. With the same stealth of his entry, he proceeded through the home's spacious two stories, and they proved innocent of intruders, as well as incriminating fireworks or hair-raising Polaroids. That done, he returned to the dining room and the shopping bag he couldn't remember being there earlier.

The bag lay beside the fruit bowl that he and Stan never used, its handles in stiff ellipses from use. Pete grew dubious as he neared: its crinkled side advertised Budd's, a crummy general store that neither he nor Stan shopped at. The overhead light described obscure shapes behind the semi-opaque plastic, along with random smears of a dark liquid. In lieu of touching the bag, Pete found a butcher knife and lifted it open.

He at first didn't understand what was inside. He distantly recognized it, but it was all wrong, there, in a bag, and his mind discombobulated. It was something he saw every day -- was quite intimate with, in fact -- but it didn't belong there, like finding cereal in your underwear drawer. Then his perception adjusted, and he gasped: the bag was filled with the calico map of Sally's coat, four little swatches of it. He threw away the knife and upended the bag over the table, emptying Sally's paws to the gleaming parquet wood. With them came a clattering rain of tawny objects, what Pete soon discerned as claws.

Shaking, he claimed one of the macabre trophies and held it to the light, Sally's familiar fur robbed of its comfort. Crusts of blood clogged the divested sockets, and once Pete understood the ramifications of this -- dead dogs neither bleed nor clot -- he returned the paws to the bag and stormed the foyer coat closet. He tore it open and produced a seasoned old baseball bat Stan kept for some inane reason.

Then he was out the door, heading across the way.

* * * * *

John Cody's house offered its usual rancor, but Pete wasn't intimidated. He wasn't much of anything, really, except enraged. Rain drenched him and he didn't notice. The pickup truck remained absent.

He tried the front door with the hand not holding the bat, and the knob remained obstinately still. Unfazed, he quit the stoop and circled the yard for the descending driveway that led to the garage. As he did so, a flash of light erupted from his back, loud and bright, like a little lightning strike. It reflected in concert from the home's many windows, making Pete jump.

He wheeled around, the bat cutting air ... but there was only his Jaguar and the dark tract of woods surrounding his house. He waited a minute, then continued down the passage.

The garage panel, too, proved locked, so he trudged up a rickety flight of steps to the mutant home's back porch, where there was another locked door and several very destructible windows. He selected the largest of the lot and, with a fantastic crash, drove the bat through. After clearing the wound, he crawled into a galactic black.

Inside was the stink of other people's cooking, and he wrinkled his nose despite himself. He hunkered there for a minute, clenching the bat and waiting on his night vision, then blindly found a light switch. The light painted him inside a conservative kitchen, between a brimming trashcan and a sink filled with soiled dishes.

"Sally!" he cried out, loud enough to rattle the dishes.

When there was no answer, he took to the premises, much as he had his own home minutes earlier. He shambled from room to room, dragging the bat limply at his side, looking for any trace of Sally or John Cody or something that could justify his breaking and entering. He burned every light as he went, numbed to care in his bereaved and sleep-deprived state. He yelled every so often, "Sally!" or "Cody!" or the pidgin of the exasperated, but the house was eerily empty, presenting a skeleton crew of dime-store furniture and little else.

The kitchen contained a prehistoric lime-green refrigerator, a gas stove, and several cupboards crammed with canned vegetables and Vienna sausage. The dining room contained a cracked wooden table with claw feet, and a lonely lyre-backed chair. In the living room was a loveseat with pan-caked cushions and a pox of faded stains. No TV, no microwave, no pictures. The other two downstairs rooms were completely empty, except for a drowsy crust of dust and spider webs that could've been there for decades.

INSOMNIA

The house was sterile of all personality, the irreligious dwelling of a non-person.

Behind the last door was a stairway leading down cellar, which Pete ignored in favor of going upstairs. There, he found two more empty rooms, followed by a bathroom and bedroom that obviously saw use. In the bedroom was a canopy bed without sheets, a debilitated mahogany dresser that looked like something from the dump, and a small writing desk that sat crooked. Pete riffled through the room, his bat knocking the warped floorboards, and then stopped as he came to the desk. On it were two boxes: one labeled **SMITH AND WESSON .44** in black cursive type, and the other, **POLAROID**. Bullets and film.

He emptied both; the first contained a Styrofoam platter of polished shells, six shy of being full. The film box was empty. Pete attacked the drawers and then the dresser, but there was nothing of note, only clothes and papers worthless to him.

The bathroom was large and dim and smelled of Man, like Dad's personal bathroom when Pete was a kid. The shower curtain was drawn, and Pete struck out at it, the plastic billowing with a screech. He checked behind it anyway, plus the half-sized closet at his back, but both were innocent of John Cody. There was a vanity, and he checked its drawers as he had the desk, but they yielded only the usual assortment of toiletries a single man would demand. Then he tried the medicine cabinet behind the mirror, and his eyebrows disappeared beneath his hair: pill bottles lined all three shelves.

There were no less than thirty in all, crammed two-deep in dental rows. Squat white bottles with flashy labels, dwarfed orange prescription bottles, slender green vials like little trees. Pete scanned the miniature dispensary, and each medication had one thing in common: they were all sleep aids.

Pete swung shut the medicine cabinet, eliciting a gunshot of pill-chatter. Back downstairs, he noticed a black rotary phone of the same ancient vintage of the refrigerator, crowning a chintzy plywood table in the hallway. He picked it up, caught a dial tone, put it down. He took one more sweep for good measure, and didn't see a bullhorn -- or *anything* incriminating, now that he thought about it. The realization sobered him some, and more followed: there was the empty box of Polaroid film, but how many people have Polaroid cameras? Millions? And the bullhorn -- couldn't it have been a trick of the baffles? Or, imagined completely?

Doubt sacked him, and the rage snuffed out. Pete took a startled look around, as if waking from a dream, and dropped the bat like it was hot, sending a belligerent wood-on-wood *thonk!* through what seemed like the entire cosmos. Sweating, he absently picked it up and began retracing his course through the house, switching off lights, righting things to the best of his recollection. He was suddenly terrified of Cody coming home -- as well as the clawing notion that the guy was innocent, that Pete had victimized some reclusive insomniac for the second time in a week.

The yawning interior grew malign as Pete traipsed through, his fear manufacturing shapes in the dark. He eventually stood in the stinking kitchen through which he'd entered, the empty window communicating with the pissing night. He killed the final light and started for home, then remembered the basement. The cellar door stood nearby, calling him, whispering of a treasure trove of damning evidence to sling at John Cody -- the bullhorn, or more Polaroids, or the rest of Sally.

The last possibility renewed the rage, and he about-faced down the hall.

A single hanging bulb illuminated the barn wood stairwell, rebuking just enough darkness to show a grayed set of risers. Halfway down, a musty odor gripped him, like mildew and old magazines. The rain dulled as he entered the bowels of the house, lending a sense of insularity that he could've done without. He felt a world apart from the rental home waiting just across the street.

The stairwell ended at a metal door, colored the same dead gray as the risers. It swung heavy on its hinges, like something from a dungeon, presumably leading to the basement garage visible from outside. The hanging light found no purchase past the jamb, and Pete again let his eyes acclimate, closing the door behind him to facilitate the process. However, the darkness was complete, and he could see nothing. A smooth cement floor lay cold beneath his feet.

Thinking fast, he fashioned Stan's baseball bat into a blind man's cane, extending it into the black and waving in broad arcs. He allowed a step for every swing, and after three swings, the bat struck something, and he knew at once it wasn't the wall he'd been gunning for. First, the bat had connected while swinging left instead of right, where the wall should be. Second, the resulting noise was a sonorous belch of metal, like someone making false thunder with a square of tin, he thought. The noise described something large just in front of him, something like a wall, but not.

Pete strafed right, and now he did find the wall, along with the rounded nub of a switch. He hit it, and light from a low ceiling flooded the room, insulting Pete's dilated pupils. Cupping a hand over his eyes, he could make out a big, boxy shape dominating the room, only a loose amalgamation of geometry to his overwhelmed organs. Then his pupils contracted, and the shape resolved into John Cody's rusted pickup truck.

Pete sucked a damp lungful of air and quailed against the plywood wall, again frightened into sobriety. He started to run, but that made noise, so he went into a mincing walk, back upstairs and into the kitchen.

Pete clenched the bat, and Cody was everywhere: in the hall at his back, in the defiled kitchen, in the gaping living room to his right. The bat collided clumsily with the phone table -- *ding!* -- and Pete yelped, no different than if a hand had found his genitals. He stopped in his tracks ... and then there was just the drumming rain and the gallop of his heart. He dried sweat from his face, making a napkin of his shirt, and continued on.

It looked as if he was home free, but then a gnawing thought gave him pause: *If Cody's truck is here, then where the hell is he?* Then, hot on that one's heels: *And why did he not answer my breaking into his house?*

Finding no answers, he unlocked the door and dove into the night.

* * * * *

The fear subsided when Pete reached the rental home without meeting his neighbor, and with that came contrition, for having infracted an innocent man's house. Then, after he rediscovered the bag of Sally on the dining room table, the contrition was joined by a jeering misery. The emotion balled into a black tumor in his head, and he sat down and cried, runners of tears melding with the residual rain. He'd screwed up bad, he knew: now he was not only a victim, but an aggressor. A call to the police was in order, both to hand over his gruesome gift and report his own trespass.

He hunted for the phone, but it wasn't on the table, or anywhere else. Then he remembered leaving it in the living room earlier that day, by the window he'd been staking out. Without turning on the light, he made for the window and its accompanying chair, where the phone slept soundly. The bat dragged unenthusiastically at his side, him forgetting it was there. However, before he could reach the phone, something caught his eye, from the sofa in the middle of the room: a small white square was propped over the middle cushion, a Polaroid.

Pete ground to a sloppy stop, like a car running out of gas. He at once remembered the cop confiscating the alarming picture he'd found in the door, and neither he nor Stan owned a Polaroid camera. The picture lay face down, and Pete stared vacantly, the fear returning full throttle. The rain beat at the roof.

He slowly grabbed the glossy stock and flipped it in his hand, trembling but not from the rain. Like his opening the grocery-store bag, the picture didn't at first make sense: it depicted an ill-lit black-brown blur, what Pete soon discerned as John Cody's house,

INSOMNIA

rising in its three-tiered slouch. The vantage was from Pete's side of the street; his driveway, maybe.

Then he noticed another thing in the picture, to the far right, just at the periphery of the frame: a hunched, stocky, back-turned figure in a windbreaker that clung wetly to his frame, carrying a stick of some kind - a baseball bat.

Pete had time to remember the anomalous strobe of light that had preceded his felony, then a voice came from his back: "I got a gun pointed at yer head, Pete Santos."

The picture slipped from Pete's hand, and he did not otherwise move.

"Drop that bat 'o yours," the voice added wearily, like a father addressing a wayward child.

Pete dropped the bat. It landed business-end first, then levered gracefully lengthwise, like a felled bowling pin.

"Turn 'round, son," said the voice. "Lemme see ya'."

Pete turned, looking oddly withdrawn. He was so tired, so sleepy. There was initially nothing, just the inchoate dark of the larger room; then an unsmiling silver revolver appeared in the incoming wedge of light, far enough to reveal a grip of bony fingers. In the dark world beyond, the light just caught a tired face, pink-hued eyes set in oily rings evocative of poison ivy.

"Yer lookin' a li'l rough there, Petey," Cody said, in a high tone that betrayed his lassitude. "Not been sleepin' well?" A stutter of animal laughter followed, cut eerily short. The gun shook a little.

Pete obediently shook his head, his eyes glued to the cyclopean bore of the gun.

"Yeah, I thought as much," Cody said. Then, darkening: "I don't sleep too well myself. Never have. Doctors say my brain's all funky, or some shit ..." The voice trailed off and the eyes lowered -- then shot back to Pete, now smoldering with hate. "Sometimes I do, though. Once in a blue moon, I'll just fall off, sleep ten, twelve hours, long as nuthin' wakes me up." The eyes clouded further.

"And I gotta have them nights, you know. Gotta. Cuz otherwise, things can get a li'l crazy." Another lunatic shout of laughter, shrill in the rafters.

Pete shifted on his feet, breath coming in fitful spurts. This was torture.

"It's been bad lately, my sleepin'," Cody went on, voice lowering in a way that made Pete's stomach churn. "I went ... oh, I don't know, must'a been three weeks without a wink." Pause. "Three weeks. Five hund'd hours, that is. Thirty thousand min'tes." A chilling smile opened within the gloom. "Thas a long time to be awake, Pete Santos. Thas a long, long, long-long time."

There was a break and Pete seized on it: "Mister Cody, please --"

"*SHUT UP!*" Cody roared, the profaned face rocking into the light. It was twisted with fatigue, like something broken and taped back together.

Pete flinched. For a second, he thought the gun had gone off. His ears buzzed.

There was a long, nervous beat of silence, and then Cody spoke: "I did get to sleep, though," he picked up quietly, as though he'd never stopped. "Must'a been last *Friday*," he added peevishly, again canting forward. The "Friday" was harsh and aspirated, almost a physical thing.

Pete flinched again.

"Last Friday ..." Cody whispered, and started moving a little, swaying from side to side like a batter anticipating a pitch. Pete's eyes followed the gun. "I did everything like normal, takin' all my pills and things, all that crap that don't do nuthin'. But somehow I just ... went off." He sounded whimsical now. "Just like that. Like God said, 'John Cody, you had enough, now have some sleep,' and off I went ..." Another elastic pause; then the eyes blinked, refreshing the bald hate written there. "*AND THEN SOME COCK FUCK SHIT SHOT A FIRECRACKER AT MUH HOUSE!*"

INSOMNIA

Pete grimaced and squinted his eyes, rappelling soggy tears down his cheeks. "I'm sorry," he said over white lips, sounding all of five. "I was drunk and I'm ... I'm sorry."

"Well, I'm sure you are, son," Cody said, hoarse from his outburst, and winded, too, as if it had siphoned his last iota of energy. "But you still gotta pay, all the same."

The hammer clicked and Pete opened his eyes, impossibly wide. Then, in one deft, horrible movement, the amorphous shape that was John Cody twirled around, sucked the gun, and fired. Blood and other ejecta sprayed Pete's face. He screamed.

Six months later

Stan Castle worked the pharmacy's friendly checkout, seeing to a patient line of customers. A cute blonde was buying tampons, pleasantly exposed in her spring dress, no doubt a co-ed from the university. Stan took her money, smiled devilishly, and then saw her on her way. As he tended to the next in line, a wrinkly little old lady, the polar opposite of his last customer, Stan noticed another body file quietly to the back of the line, a man. Only as the line cleared did Stan recognize him as Pete Santos.

Stan grew at once uncomfortable, as the healthy do when sensing sickness. "Hey, Pete," he said, a little too passionately. "Long time no see." Stan had moved out after the incident, and hadn't seen Pete since.

"Hey, yeah ..." Pete wheezed, sounding like he'd just taken one in the gut.

Stan tried to meet Pete's eyes, but it was impossible. Pete looked beyond bad, all sallow and wilted; with a ghoulish look in his eyes -- understandable, considering he'd taken a bath in some freak's brains, or so Stan had heard. There was a wasted attitude about him, like clabbered milk, or a junked car oxidizing in someone's yard. Pete had lost a considerable amount of weight, leaving him with a sick excess of skin, shriveled like the distensible throat of a toad. Wearing a sweaty white tee-shirt that was far too big for him, he looked to be swaddled in a sheet.

There was an awkward silence, and the thing that was Pete flaccidly presented his purchase, a colorful box of Super Sleep PM.

"Can't sleep?" Stan asked, and instantly felt stupid: it was like asking a guy on a respirator to whistle "Yankee Doodle". He swiped the box over the barcode reader, kicking himself in the ass.

INSOMNIA

Pete said something that sounded like "No," then produced a few crumpled bills without Stan asking for them. Stan made change and bagged up the pills, then hazarded a look into Pete's crippled eyes. Pete stared at the counter.

"Good to see you," Stan said noncommittally, sliding over the bag.

Pete didn't look up. "Yeah," he said, and then left the pharmacy.

A. A. Garrison is a twenty-seven-year-old man living in the mountains of western North Carolina, writing and landscaping. His work has recently appeared in Inkspill Magazine and the anthology Rotting Tales.